No Way Out . . .

Something gleamed among the scraps of paper and pencils and tape in the drawer. Something shiny and black.

A gun.

Adam reached around Carter and picked up the pistol. She stared at him in shock.

"Like it?" he asked her.

Carter was shaking now. She was alone in a house on Fear Street with a guy who had a gun.

Books by R. L. Stine

HOW I BROKE UP
  WITH ERNIE
PHONE CALLS
CURTAINS
BROKEN DATE

Fear Street Cheerleaders

THE FIRST EVIL
THE SECOND EVIL
THE THIRD EVIL

Fear Street Super Chiller

PARTY SUMMER
SILENT NIGHT
GOODNIGHT KISS
BROKEN HEARTS

Fear Street

THE NEW GIRL
THE SURPRISE PARTY
THE OVERNIGHT
MISSING
THE WRONG NUMBER
THE SLEEPWALKER
HAUNTED
HALLOWEEN PARTY
THE STEPSISTER
SKI WEEKEND
THE FIRE GAME
LIGHTS OUT
THE SECRET BEDROOM
THE KNIFE
PROM QUEEN
FIRST DATE
THE BEST FRIEND
THE CHEATER

Available from ARCHWAY Paperbacks

FEAR STREET®
R·L·STINE

The Cheater

AN ARCHWAY PAPERBACK
Published by POCKET BOOKS
New York   London   Toronto   Sydney   Tokyo   Singapore

AN ARCHWAY PAPERBACK *Original*

An Archway Paperback published by
POCKET BOOKS, a division of Simon & Schuster Inc.
1230 Avenue of the Americas, New York, NY 10020

ISBN: 0-671-73867-4

First Archway Paperback printing April 1993

10 9 8 7 6 5 4 3

Cover art by Bill Schmidt

Printed in the U.S.A.

IL 7+

chapter

1

The first time Carter Phillips thought about cheating, it was a joke. Carter had never cheated in her life.

Later that day she surprised herself by thinking about it seriously. Am I desperate enough to cheat? she wondered.

And the frightening answer came back: *Yes.*

As she sat in advanced math class, chin in hand, her silky white-blond hair hanging veil-like in front of her face, she stared at Mr. Raub standing behind his desk.

Why had she ever thought she could do advanced math?

"Just a reminder," said the math teacher. He was a pale, thin, bald man with a brown mustache. "If any of you want to take the math achievement test again, it's being given Saturday at Waynesbridge Junior College. It's a chance to improve your score.

But most of you guys did okay the first time, I'm happy to say."

The bell rang. Carter sighed and picked up her books. She was joined by her boyfriend, Dan Mason, and her best friend, Jill Bancroft. The three of them made their way out of the classroom together.

Jill flipped her long brown hair over her shoulder and turned to Carter with sympathy. "Do you *really* have to take it again?" she asked. "I mean, your score was better than mine, and *I'm* not taking it on Saturday."

"You don't have to live with my father," Carter said with a sigh. "Judge Carter. Who judges all the time."

Carter's father was a criminal court judge in Shadyside. She was very proud of him—she knew that people admired him, that he had a lot of influence in town. More than anything, Carter wanted to please her father, but it wasn't always easy. He had very high standards, and he expected Carter, his only child, to live up to them.

Carter's father used to tell her how proud he was of her almost every day, but something had gone wrong.

Carter was a very good student, but her weakest subject was math. She remembered the exact day, a few months earlier. Her math achievement test scores had just arrived in the mail. Judge Phillips stood watching over her shoulder as she opened the envelope.

She looked at the score—570. Not bad, she thought, pleased with herself. Not bad for math. . . .

She turned around to show the score to her father, but saw that he had already seen it. She could tell by his face that she'd been wrong: evidently 570 was *not* a good score.

Frowning, the judge crossed his arms over his chest and said, "Well, Carter, I guess you'll have to take it over again. You can't get into Princeton with a math score like that." He turned and strode back into his study, shutting the door behind him.

Carter's heart sank. She'd always been able to please her father—she'd won tennis tournaments, school prizes, and made honor roll every year—but now she couldn't.

Her father had graduated from Princeton, and he'd talked about sending Carter there as long as she could remember. She'd never even asked herself whether she wanted to go to Princeton. It had always been a given.

Now it appeared that something stood in her way—advanced math. One little test score was keeping her from being successful, keeping her from fulfilling her father's dream.

It didn't seem fair.

Carter had tried her best, but this time her best wasn't good enough.

Carter's mother came into the living room just after the judge had shut himself in his study. Carter was still standing with the test results in her hand, her head hanging down.

Mrs. Phillips didn't even ask Carter about her test scores. She just glanced at the closed study door and said, "Honey, I'm late for the Hospital Fund meeting. Tell your father I'll be home around six, will you?" She kissed Carter on the forehead and breezed out the door with a clatter of jewelry.

Carter stared after her in a daze. She realized she'd have to take the math test over. She'd have to study and study. There was no way out of it.

Deep down, she knew it wouldn't help. She'd never get the score she needed, not in a million years.

Now Dan put his arm around Carter's shoulders as they walked through the hall at school. "It won't be so bad, Carter," he said. "Just a few hours on Saturday and it'll be over forever."

Carter looked up at her tall, good-looking boyfriend and tried to smile.

"I don't mind retaking the test—not too much anyway," she said. "That's not the problem. The problem is that Daddy expects me to score at least seven hundred—and I know I can't do it. I studied my brains out the first time I took the test. I've been studying hard this time too, but it's hopeless! You have to be practically a genius to get a seven hundred—and I'm no math genius."

4

Dan sighed. Carter knew he felt uncomfortable about this. He was great at math, and had scored 720 on the test. But he was a modest guy, and he didn't want Carter to feel bad about it. So he changed the subject.

"What you need is a milk shake. My treat. Let's go to The Corner." He turned to Jill and asked, "Want to come?"

Jill shook her head. "I can't. I've got a photography club meeting. Try to cheer up, Carter. See you later."

"Bye, Jill."

Now that Jill was gone, Carter let herself lean over and rest against Dan's shoulder. They stepped outside into a damp, breezy, warm spring day, unusually warm for March.

They walked the few blocks to The Corner, a coffee shop and hangout for kids from Shadyside High. It was busy—all the booths were taken. Dan and Carter had to settle for the counter and ordered chocolate milk shakes.

Dan reached down the counter for a copy of *Car Talk* lying there. "Some motor head must have left it," he said, flipping the pages. He stopped at a photo spread of luxury cars and asked Carter, "If you could have any of these cars, which would you pick?"

It was a game they often played. Carter and Dan would drive down a block in their fancy North Hills neighborhood and ask each other which house they'd pick if they could have any one they wanted.

Or they'd flip through a magazine and ask each other which outfit they'd pick, or which models they liked the best, or what island they'd go to, if they could go anywhere.

Carter wasn't really in the mood for the game, but she dutifully looked over the cars and pointed to a blue Jaguar.

"I think I'd pick the BMW," said Dan.

Carter didn't look at the BMW. She was absentmindedly watching as the waiters and waitresses changed shifts. Adam Messner, who was in their advanced math class, took an apron from a hook and tied it around his narrow waist. He was starting his shift behind the counter.

Dan's hand covered hers, and she turned back to him, to his handsome face, his jaunty smile, straight brown hair, and kind green eyes. Good old Dan. He'd always been there for her.

He was acting concerned. "Still worrying about your test?" he asked her.

She nodded. "Things are so tense at home," she told him. "You know my dad, he always has a lot on his mind. But now, with the Austin case and reporters hounding him, he comes home from court every day in a terrible mood."

Everyone in Shadyside knew about the Austin case. Henry Austin was a notorious gang leader who'd been arrested for murder. The press couldn't get enough of the story, and Judge Phillips, who hated publicity, was presiding over the case.

"Mom's no help," Carter went on. "Sometimes I

6

think all her chatter about her charity balls and committee meetings makes Dad edgier. She lives in her own little world. It's as if she wants to ignore all the tension in the house, pretend it isn't there."

Carter glanced up at Dan. He nodded and squeezed her hand, encouraging her to say more.

"And then I come along with my stupid math problem. Dan, there's no way I can get a seven hundred on this test. I took a practice test just last week and I only scored six hundred. Dad's going to go through the roof if I don't do better than that."

She sighed and lowered her head, letting her hair fall over her face. "If only I could borrow your brain on Saturday, just for one day—"

She stopped suddenly and raised her eyes to meet Dan's. She tucked her hair behind her ears.

"Hey," she said, half-laughing. "You could get a seven hundred again, easily. Maybe you could take the test for me. I mean, Carter *could* be a boy's name. . . ."

She let the sentence trail off when she saw Dan's expression. His smile faded. He frowned.

Carter felt her face grow hot. She knew she was blushing. How could she have said such a thing?

"Hey, come on, Dan, I was just kidding," she said. She poked him in the ribs and pretended to be offended that he could have thought she was serious.

His face relaxed a bit. "Yeah, I knew you were kidding," he said nervously.

Carter pretended to believe him.

7

Dan slurped the last of his milk shake and glanced at his watch. "I've got to go," he said. "Mom wants me to pick her up at the tennis club. Want a ride home?"

"No thanks," said Carter. "I'm going to meet Jill at the mall in a little while."

Dan stood up and kissed her on the cheek. "Don't worry about the test. I know you'll come through."

She smiled at him. "Sure," she said. "See you tomorrow."

He kissed her again, turned, and made his way out of the restaurant.

She watched him walk out the door. Staying a minute longer, she stared at the counter and sipped her milk shake.

Dan was the greatest—sort of. He was so honest, so straight. She liked that about him, but it bothered her at the same time.

Carter was good too, basically. But sometimes she had an urge to do something just a little bad. Dan was always there to stop her, to keep her sensible and honest, to make her feel guilty for thinking about *it*, whatever *it* was.

She pushed her glass away and glanced up. Adam Messner was smiling at her across the counter.

How long had he been watching her?

Carter shifted nervously under his gaze. That smile—there was something behind it. Had he heard her talking to Dan? Had he been listening?

Adam slowly leaned across the counter toward Carter, leaned in close. "I'll do it," he whispered.

She started and pulled back from him. "What do you mean? Do what?" She knew what he meant.

"The test," he said. "I'll take it for you."

She studied his face—a lean, dark-eyed face under longish black hair. He wasn't smiling now. He was serious.

Adam was not a friend of Carter's. He lived in a shabby house on Fear Street, and he hung out with a rough crowd. But he was brilliant at math, Carter knew.

I shouldn't do it, she thought. It wouldn't be right.

But even as she thought this, she knew she wanted to. She thought of her father, how disappointed he'd be when he saw her new score—no better, maybe even worse, than the first.

No, she thought. I *have* to get a seven hundred. I'll do it.

I'll cheat.

She nodded at Adam. She knew he understood.

"Why are you doing this for me?" she whispered.

"The way I see it," he said, moving in close to her, his lips almost brushing her ear, "I've got something you want—and you've got something I want."

9

"W-what is it?" Carter stammered. "What do you want?"

Adam rested his head in his hands, elbows on the counter. "You have to go out with me," he said. "One date."

One date? Carter thought. That's all?

She relaxed. All she had to do was go on one date with Adam, and her test problem would be over.

Or would it? Could it really be that easy to cheat on the test?

"What if they ask for ID or something?" Carter whispered. "What if they find out what we're doing?"

"They won't," Adam replied confidently. "I took the test at Waynesbridge the last time. It's in this huge auditorium filled with hundreds of kids. Nobody checks IDs or anything. It'll be a piece of cake."

He's got it all figured out, Carter thought. It

really might work. Dan would be upset if he found out—but he *won't* find out.

Carter was pretty, and she knew how to handle guys. She'd go out with Adam once, get rid of him, and not tell a soul about it. It was almost too easy.

This thought made her pause. She studied Adam again. She'd never realized before that he was interested in her—she'd never even given him much thought.

Now that she was looking at him, she couldn't help but think he was cute, in a dark, brooding way. He didn't have Dan's all-American good looks, but he had something Dan didn't have—an air of mystery, a sexy kind of daring. He was standing behind the counter now, meeting her gaze, slouching, cool as ever.

"All right," she said. "One date."

Now he smiled—just a little. "Let's make it Saturday, the night of the test."

"I can't," Carter said. "I have a date that night. With Dan."

"Break it," Adam replied.

She raised her eyebrows in surprise. But she knew she'd break her date with Dan. Just this once.

Another thought occurred to her. "What is Sheila going to say about this?" she asked Adam.

Sheila Coss was Adam's girlfriend. Carter didn't know Sheila well, but she'd always felt a little afraid of her. She was tough and didn't mind getting into fights.

Adam said, "What Sheila doesn't know won't hurt her."

Carter nodded. "Well, I'd better get out of here. See you."

She waited for Adam to reply. Instead he picked up a rag and started wiping up.

Carter woke up with a start on Saturday morning and looked at her clock—eight A.M. She quickly got dressed. She had to pretend to be going to Waynesbridge.

Her father was already shut up in his study when she went downstairs to grab a glass of juice. Mrs. Phillips was on her way out the door.

"What are you doing up so early?" she asked Carter.

"I'm taking the math achievement test today," Carter said. "Remember?"

"Oh, that's right. Well, good luck, dear. I'm off to the country club. The Spring Fling is almost here, and we've still got so much planning to do!"

She threw her daughter a quick kiss and hurried out the door.

Carter finished her juice and left. She got into her car and drove toward Waynesbridge. But she passed the Waynesbridge exit and continued on to the nearby state park instead. She parked under some leafless trees and sat in the car, waiting.

Staring at the clock on the dashboard. Nine. Adam would be starting the test.

Carter felt her stomach knot up. I hope everything goes okay, she thought.

I hope he really shows up and takes it. I hope no one catches him. I hope they don't ask him for ID. I hope no one recognizes him. I hope I don't get caught. . . .

Three hours later she started the car and drove home. Her mother was still out, her father still locked up in his study.

Carter checked the answering machine for messages. There had been no calls. She wanted to hear from Adam, to know what had happened.

She was sitting in the kitchen when her father came to get his lunch. He looked tired, but he smiled when he saw her. "Carter, you're back! I didn't hear you come in."

She felt her face grow warm. To hide her blushing, she went to the refrigerator and started digging through the shelves. "Hi, Daddy. Can I fix you a sandwich?"

Judge Phillips sat down at the kitchen table. "How did the test go?"

"Great," said Carter. "I think I really aced it this time."

"I'm glad to hear it. I knew you could do better."

Carter's face reddened even more, but the judge didn't notice. She busied herself making him a ham sandwich. She was just dropping it on a plate when the phone rang. She nearly jumped.

"I'll get it!" she cried, running to the phone. "Hello?"

"Hello, Melanie?"

Melanie was Carter's mother. "This is her daughter," Carter said. "She's out right now. May I take a message?"

She jotted down a message from the woman, who was one of her mother's friends. Then she hung up. Her father was nibbling the sandwich and reading the front page of the newspaper.

The headline caught Carter's eye.

NUMBER TWO MAN IN AUSTIN GANG

TESTIFIES AGAINST BOSS—

ADMITS TO MURDERS, BRIBERY, FRAUD

That's Daddy's case, Carter thought.

"I think I'll go upstairs and take a nap," Carter said. "I'm pretty tired."

"Go ahead, honey," said her dad. "You deserve it."

She went upstairs and shut herself in her room. She had her own phone there. She dialed Adam's number.

He answered.

"Adam!" said Carter. Her heart was beating fast. "It's Carter. How did it go?"

"Beautiful," said Adam. "It was a breeze."

14

Carter breathed a sigh of relief.

Then Adam added, "Until I tried to leave."

Her heart froze. "What happened?"

"They asked everyone for photo ID. Sorry, Carter. They were ready for us."

Carter squeezed her eyes shut. This is it, she thought. I've been caught cheating. My life is over.

chapter

3

"*H*ey, Carter," said Adam. "You still there?"

Carter struggled to catch her breath. Finally she choked out, "Yes. I'm here."

The line went silent. Then Carter heard Adam making some kind of noise. It took her a moment to realize he was laughing.

Laughing!

"What are you laughing at?" she asked in a trembling voice. Did he really think this was funny?

"I was just teasing you, Carter," said Adam. "No one asked me for ID. No one suspected a thing. The test went perfectly. We're in the clear."

Carter struggled to choke back her anger. How could he joke about something so serious?

Then she realized what was behind his joke: a message. This test was serious to her, but not to him. While he had nothing to lose, her whole future was at stake.

"Now," said Adam. "It's time to collect my payment. What time should I pick you up?"

"Don't come here," Carter replied quickly. She didn't want anyone to see Adam pull up to her house—especially her parents. "I mean, you don't have to pick me up. I'll meet you somewhere."

"All right. Where?"

Carter nibbled a fingernail as she thought about it. "How about the corner of Village Road and Mission Street?" This was in the Old Village, several blocks from her house. "Do you know where that is?"

"Sure," said Adam. "I'll meet you there at eight."

"Good."

"And, Carter, try not to dress like a North Hills princess. We're going into *my* world tonight and it's no country club." He hung up before Carter could say a word.

Carter was seething. How *dare* he call her a princess? She could handle any place he wanted to take her.

Still, while dressing for the date later that evening, she was careful about what she wore. She put on a pair of ripped jeans and a plain black top. She took off all her jewelry.

At five minutes to eight she left the house, telling her mother that she was going to Jill's. She walked two blocks, then took the bus to Village and Mission—and waited.

Five minutes later a beat-up old black Mustang pulled up to the corner and stopped. It was Adam.

He didn't turn off the motor and get out of the car. He just stuck his head out the window and gave Carter a sexy smile. "Hi," he said. "Get in."

She walked around the car to the passenger side. He flipped the door open and she slid in.

They rode in silence. Awkward silence.

Every few minutes Carter glanced at Adam, trying not to let him see she was studying him.

She couldn't help thinking that he looked great. He wore jeans and a plaid shirt—nothing special, but on his lean frame they had an easy sexiness.

In the same clothes, Dan would have looked neat and buttoned-up, somehow. But with his shaggy hair and dark eyes, Adam was almost a rock star.

Carter watched as they rolled through the Old Village. "Where are we going?" she asked him.

"The Underground. Ever been there?"

"No—not yet." Carter didn't want to admit that she'd never even heard of it.

They were slowly cruising through a seedy warehouse district. The streets were deserted, lit only by an occasional street lamp. They turned down a dark alley and Carter noticed a lot of cars parked outside one of the warehouses. There was no sign —just a red light over the door.

Adam pulled into a small clear area. Carter knew that this was it—the Underground.

Without a backward glance at Carter, Adam climbed out of the car and started toward the door with the red light over it. Carter followed him.

Adam pulled open the door. Carter was suddenly hit by a blast of loud music. A brawny bouncer stood just inside. He glanced at Adam and checked Carter out, but he didn't stop them.

The club was huge, dark, and crowded. Some people sat in a corner, smoking and talking. Others were crammed in the center of the room, dancing.

Most of the guys had Adam's careless, slightly dangerous look—uncombed long hair, scruffy clothes, combat boots. The girls wore jeans or tight dresses, dark lipstick, and sneering expressions.

Carter knew she didn't fit in, no matter how hard she had tried not to dress "like a North Hills princess." Her jeans were torn at the knee but clean, her blond hair neatly trimmed. Her skin had a pampered glow. She felt a little uneasy as she glanced around the club and saw hostile glares in the eyes of some of the girls.

But knowing she was out of place comforted her too. At least, she thought, I won't run into anybody I know. As Adam had said, the Underground was no country club.

Adam took her hand and led her through the crowd onto the dance floor. They started moving to the pounding beat. Adam was the first guy she'd ever danced with who didn't look stupid while he danced. He moved loosely, with cool detachment. He danced in his own little world, but once in a while he gazed at her with burning eyes and gave her that smile.

The music went on and on without stopping, one song moving seamlessly into another. Carter found herself getting lost in it. She forgot about the people all around her and just danced.

She glanced up at Adam and found him staring at her while she moved. They locked eyes and danced together, without touching.

The room grew more crowded. People bumped into them, pushed them closer, but it was all part of the music and the beat. The club was getting hotter, the music even louder.

Carter didn't know how long she danced. She felt a drop of sweat slide down her back.

The crowd had thinned a little when Adam took her hand again and pulled her off the dance floor. He stopped at a table and asked for two glasses of water.

Carter drank the water quickly. She was very thirsty. Her face and hair were now damp with sweat. She was having a good time. It surprised her.

"Let's go," Adam said. He put his glass on the table, pulled hers out of her hand, and set it down too. Then he led her to the door.

Outside, the air was cool. Carter smiled and said, "It feels great out here!"

Adam unbuttoned his shirt and fanned it around his body to cool himself off. "You're a good dancer," he said.

Carter blushed a little. "So are you."

She glanced around, looking for the black Mustang. A lot of cars were gone. It must be later than I realized, she thought.

She slid into Adam's car, and he drove her through the quiet, late-night streets. Carter rolled down her window and let the spring breeze cool her face. The radio played softly.

At last they turned onto her street. She told Adam to let her off at the corner. Adam pulled over to the curb. Carter couldn't help but feel the night was over too soon.

She turned to him to thank him, but she had just managed to open her mouth when he leaned over and kissed her, long and hard.

At first she was surprised, but then she lost herself in it, just as she'd lost herself in the music at the Underground.

When it was over, Carter found herself gasping for breath.

Finally she said awkwardly, "Thanks for everything, Adam. Thanks for—you know—the test, and the date too."

She opened her door and climbed out. As she closed the door behind her, he called out through the open window, "What are you doing tomorrow?"

She stopped. The next day was Sunday. "Tomorrow?" she said. "I'm playing tennis with Jill at one at the club—if it's warm enough."

"Great," said Adam. "I'll meet you there at one."

He *what!*

This stopped Carter cold.

One date, she thought. We agreed on one date.

But before she had a chance to object, Adam sped off down the street. She watched his taillights disappear around the corner. He was gone.

She hurried down the dark street toward her house.

How had she gotten herself into this? What would she do with a guy like Adam at the North Hills Country Club? He'd fit in there even less than she fit in at the Underground.

And how would she explain it to Jill? Jill didn't know about the test or the date. No one did.

And no one would. That was the most important thing of all.

Adam couldn't have been serious, Carter thought. He doesn't really want to go to the club. He was just teasing me. Another joke.

Soon she convinced herself that Adam didn't mean to go to the club at all. She should have felt better, but the street was so eerily quiet, so empty and dark. . . .

She quickened her pace, glancing warily into the shadows all around her. The yellow light burned beside her front door—just a few more feet.

She walked up the front path. Don't worry, she told herself. You're almost home. You're almost safe. . . .

Then suddenly something moved in the bushes next to the house.

Carter froze. What was that?

She stared at the bushes, but they were still. Then they stirred again.

Carter was too frightened to run.

A figure moved in the shadows.

"It's about time you got home," a voice said nastily. "I've been waiting for you."

THE CHAPTER

chapter

4

Carter wanted to run, but her legs felt as heavy as lead.

"Who's there?" she cried in a whisper.

The figure moved into the light. Carter squinted, trying to focus on who it was.

It was a woman. No. A girl. Skinny, with pale red hair.

Carter recognized her. It was Sheila Coss. Adam's girlfriend.

"Sheila? What are you doing here?"

Sheila stood between Carter and the door. "What's going on between you and Adam?" she snapped.

How did Sheila know about that? Carter wondered. Maybe she didn't really know anything. Maybe she was just guessing. Carter decided the only thing to do was lie.

"I don't know what you're talking about," Carter said. "I hardly even know Adam."

24

Sheila gave a little laugh, a cynical "hah." She pulled a pack of cigarettes from her back pocket, lit one, and frowned at Carter.

"I know Adam's been sneaking around with some other girl," she said. "I've known it for weeks now."

Carter hid her surprise. Was it true? She wondered who else had Adam been seeing?

She watched as Sheila paused to blow a smoke ring into the night air. She's just paranoid, Carter thought. That must be it.

Sheila went on. "The only thing I don't know— not for certain, anyway—is *who* the little rat has been seeing. But I'm going to find out. Soon."

The air was starting to feel chilly on Carter's damp skin. It was late, and she was tired. She wanted to go inside.

She made a move toward the door. Sheila blocked her way.

"If it's you, Carter," Sheila said in a nasty whisper, "you better hope I don't find out about it. 'Cause when I find the girl, she's going to wish she never laid eyes on Adam."

She stepped out of Carter's path now, tossing her cigarette on the lawn. Then she moved away, casually, as if she had all the time in the world.

Carter stamped out the cigarette and hurried into the house. She shut the door behind her and locked it, her hands shaking.

She made her way to her room and undressed for bed. But once in bed, she couldn't relax. "The test is over now," she told herself, trying to calm her nerves. "The date is over. It's all over. And Sheila doesn't know anything for sure—"

But if Sheila didn't know anything, what had made her show up at Carter's house that night? What would make her suspect that Carter was seeing Adam, unless she knew *something?*

With these thoughts whirling through her mind, Carter eventually managed to fall into a restless sleep.

She woke up late the next day, still tired. If she didn't dress quickly, she'd be late for her tennis date with Jill.

She threw on a clean white T-shirt and a pair of white shorts, and grabbed her tennis racket, bag, and car keys.

She pulled into the club parking lot at exactly one. The sun was bright, and the air was very warm. So far it had been a very early spring.

Carter got out of the car and started for the clubhouse, looking for Jill's car. It wasn't there.

But Adam was.

He was standing outside the gates, wearing a black T-shirt, cutoff jeans, and black high-top sneakers—not exactly proper tennis attire. His dark hair was pulled back in a ponytail, and he was holding a beat-up wooden tennis racquet and a gym bag.

Adam was scowling. A uniformed security guard stood next to him, his arms folded across his chest.

Carter gulped nervously as she walked toward the gates. He was serious, she thought. He really showed up. I can't believe it!

"Hi, Carter," Adam said when she reached him. "This guy"—he jerked his thumb toward the guard —"wouldn't let me in. I told him I'm your guest, but he doesn't believe me."

Carter wanted to sink into the ground. The guard stared at her, slightly surprised now. But his face didn't completely lose its no-nonsense expression.

"Um, it's okay," she said to the guard. "He's with me."

The guard, still skeptical, let his arms drop from his chest and stepped aside.

Carter led Adam through the gate into North Hills Country Club.

North Hills was the most exclusive club in Shadyside. High walls hid it from public view, so few nonmembers even knew what it was like. Inside, the grounds were beautifully landscaped. There were two heated pools, plush locker rooms, ten perfectly kept tennis courts, and a rolling green golf course.

The clubhouse was an old Tudor-style mansion. Inside, there were squash and racquetball courts, a banquet hall lit by a huge crystal chandelier, lounges filled with leather-covered furniture, and a restaurant overlooking the practice green.

Carter had belonged to North Hills all her life and had always taken all this luxury for granted. To her it was just "the club."

But now, as she led Adam across the grounds to the snack bar, she noticed people staring at them. Darkly dressed Adam stood out among all the perfectly groomed preppies lounging about in their white tennis clothes.

At the same time Carter tried to imagine how the club must look to Adam, an outsider all his life. Thinking of it made her feel very uncomfortable.

The place must seem pretty stuffy to him, she thought. And all the people a bunch of stuck-up bores.

She gave him a stiff smile as they sat at one of the wicker tables in the snack bar to wait for Jill. Some people at a table nearby appeared to be talking about him. Adam didn't seem to notice.

"You looked surprised to see me," Adam said to Carter.

She shifted uncomfortably. "No, I wasn't surprised. Really."

He gave a low laugh. "Yes, you were. It was written all over your face."

She was glad to see Jill striding quickly toward them—it meant she could change the subject.

As Jill drew closer, Carter saw confusion on her face. She's recognized Adam, Carter thought, and she doesn't understand what he's doing here. What will I tell her?

"Hi, Jill," Carter said before Jill had a chance to open her mouth. "You know Adam Messner from math class, right?"

"Sure," Jill said. "But—"

28

Carter interrupted her. "He's going to play tennis with us. Now we just need a fourth for doubles."

"I'll join you," said a voice. It belonged to a tall, good-looking blond guy sitting at the table next to Carter's.

Her heart sank when she saw who it was. Richard Smith.

Richard Smith was cute, but extremely snooty—too snobbish and uptight for Carter's crowd. He had been trying to get Carter to go out with him since ninth grade, but Carter wouldn't go. She enjoyed turning him down time after time, though nothing she did seemed to squash his giant ego. He kept coming back for more.

Richard stood up and sauntered over to Carter's table. He looked down his long, perfect nose at Adam.

Adam coolly ignored him. Carter couldn't help feeling a little proud of Adam, in a perverse way. She was glad Richard didn't ruffle him. Adam could hold his own.

"I like your ponytail," Richard said with a smirk.

"Shut up, Richard," Carter said. "You and Jill against me and Adam. Let's go."

They went down to the courts. Adam served first. He aced it.

"I wasn't ready yet," Richard complained. "But I'll let that one go."

Jill returned Adam's next serve, but Adam and Carter won the point anyway.

29

The game quickly became intense. Carter found herself concentrating hard and really enjoying the game. Together, she and Adam were making Jill and Richard run. Sweat was pouring off Richard's face.

Adam, with his funky clothes and wooden racquet, was a skilled player. His style was aggressive, and he blew Richard off the court.

Carter and Adam won the match.

Richard stormed off the court without a word.

Jill came around the net and said, "Great game, guys. Sorry Richard was such a bad sport."

Carter smiled at Adam. "I don't think Richard expected to lose. Where did you learn to play tennis so well?"

"At the public tennis courts," said Adam. "My older brother taught me." Adam gave Carter his slow grin. She felt her face get warm.

"Let's go shower," said Jill. "I've got to get home soon."

Carter pointed out the men's locker room to Adam. She and Jill went into the women's.

As soon as the door closed behind them, Jill cornered Carter. "I've been dying to ask you all afternoon," she said. *"What's* going on? What's Adam doing here?"

The excitement of the tennis game faded quickly. Carter's stomach began to rumble nervously. She forgot for a moment why she was with Adam in the first place—because she had to be. Because he knew her secret.

But Carter was determined not to let Jill find out. She tried to bluff her way out of this.

"I ran into Adam on my way here," she said, shrugging. "He was hanging around outside the club, and I thought it would be sort of a good deed to invite him in."

Jill seemed to be skeptical. "A good deed? You never gave Adam the time of day before."

"I know," said Carter. "Maybe I was wrong. I'd hate to be as big a snob as Richard is. And Adam really showed him up, didn't he?"

Jill giggled. "For sure. I have to admit, that was a hoot—even if I was on the losing side."

Now, thought Carter, it's time to change the subject. She definitely didn't want to talk about Adam anymore.

"So, how was your date last night?" Carter asked. "I can't believe you haven't even mentioned it yet!"

Jill had gone out with Gary Brandt the night before. She smiled when Carter brought it up.

"It was great," she said happily. "I didn't want to talk about it in front of the guys, but I really like him. We've only gone out three times, but I've got a good feeling about Gary. He's so sweet!" Her face was glowing. "I think this could be the real thing— like you and Dan."

At that, Carter had to turn away. The real thing, she thought. Me and Dan.

Adam's face kept appearing in her mind. She tried to push the image away, but it was stubborn. It stayed.

31

Jill slammed her locker shut. "I've got to go," she said. "Mom's having people over tonight and I promised I'd help her." She picked up her tennis bag and said, "See you tomorrow."

Carter felt a twinge of envy as she watched Jill hurry from the locker room, her brown ponytail bouncing.

She seems so carefree, Carter thought. She has nothing more to worry about than dates with a nice guy and helping her mother with a party. And she thinks my life is just the same. If only she knew what I've been doing lately. . . .

Carter sighed and finished dressing. She left the club a few minutes later.

Just outside the gates she found Adam waiting for her. He was freshly showered, wearing a clean pair of jeans and a white T-shirt, his hair slicked back. Carter smiled at him.

"You were great today," she said. "I've been trying to find a way to show up Richard Smith for years. Thanks."

They walked into the parking lot. Adam stopped and leaned against his black Mustang.

"I know a better way you can thank me," he said. "Go out with me again."

Carter didn't know what to say. Another date. Part of her wanted to go. But Dan . . .

"Friday night," Adam said. "I'll pick you up at the same corner."

"Friday night!" said Carter. Now she knew she couldn't go. She'd promised Dan—and she'd already broken one date with him to go out with Adam. She wouldn't do it again.

"I can't do it Friday, Adam," she said. She was shocked to hear a pleading note in her voice. How had she come to this—pleading with a boy like Adam?

Adam sighed. He moved around to the door of his car and got in. He started the motor.

Carter stood by nervously. Why didn't he say anything? She stood near the open window of his car.

Now Adam spoke very calmly.

"If you really want to go," he said, "you'll find a way. And if I were you, Carter, I'd want to keep me happy. Know what I mean?"

He pulled out of the parking lot, tires throwing up gravel behind them.

Carter stood there a moment, totally alone.

Adam was right. She had to keep him happy.

And she knew it.

But for how long?

chapter

5

Carter was surprised to find her father already home when she got back from school. It was Wednesday afternoon. Judge Phillips was sitting in his study, with the door open.

Carter stood in the doorway with her schoolbooks in her arms. "Hi, Daddy. Is the case finished?"

The judge smiled wryly. "Hardly. The courtroom was so tense that I had to call a recess this afternoon to let things cool down. That Henry Austin—he has no shame. During testimony this morning, he stood up and started threatening the witnesses. I had to order him out of the courtroom."

Now Judge Phillips beckoned to his daughter. "Enough about that. Come in and sit down," he said. "I want to speak with you."

Carter went into the study and sat in the leather

armchair on the other side of her father's desk. She waited to hear what he had to say.

"Princeton needs your latest math score as soon as possible don't they?" he asked. "They'll be making final decisions this month. What if I call the testing service right now and ask for your score? Then we can be sure Princeton will have it in time."

Carter tried to hide her nervousness by squeezing her notebooks with her hands—hard. She swallowed before she spoke, to help steady her voice.

"Good idea, Daddy. Call them. I can't wait to find out how I did."

The judge put on his glasses and reached for the telephone. "I've got the number right here," he muttered.

He dialed. Carter squeezed her books and shut her eyes.

Please, she prayed, please let everything be okay.

She hardly dared to think of all the things that could have gone wrong. What if Adam purposely messed up on the test?

No, he wouldn't do that, but he might not have done as well as he thought he had.

Carter knew her father would be satisfied with nothing less than 700. She could imagine what would happen if she scored lower than that.

He'd tell her to close the door. Then what? He'd make it clear that he was disappointed. He'd tell her that her life was ruined—and she'd ruined his too.

But the worst possibility of all was much more terrible than that. What if the testing service said that they suspected that Carter had cheated?

What if, somehow, they *knew?*

"This is Judge John Phillips," she heard her father say. "My daughter, Carter, took the math achievement test for the second time last Saturday. We need to send the score to Princeton right away. Would it be possible for you to give it to us early?"

He paused. Then he put his hand over the receiver. "They're going to give us the score now, over the phone," he whispered.

Carter's knuckles went white. In her lap, out of her father's sight, her hands were shaking. She gave him a queasy smile.

"Yes, I'm here. Phillips. Two *l*'s. That's right."

There was another pause. Carter could hardly stand it. If they don't hurry up and give him the score I'll go crazy, she thought.

"Yes. Yes. Uh-huh. Thank you. Thank you very much."

Judge Phillips put down the phone, his face grave.

"Daddy?" said Carter. "What did they say?"

Her father stood up. Carter stared at him in horror as he moved around the desk toward her.

What had they told him?

"Carter," he began, "I have never been as proud of you as I am at this moment."

Proud? He was proud? Her mind was whirling. That must be good—right?

36

He stood by her chair now and took both her hands in his. "Carter, you can relax. Your score was seven thirty!"

Now he broke into a wide smile. It was a few seconds before Carter understood what he had said. 730! She got a 730! Everything was all right.

Judge Phillips pulled her up from her seat. Her books fell from her lap to the floor, but he didn't notice. He spun her around and around.

"Princeton, here she comes!" he cried joyfully.

Carter started to laugh. She had rarely seen her father so happy.

At last he stopped twirling and said, "Hurry upstairs and tell your mother the good news. I've just got to run an errand. I won't be long!"

He rushed out. Carter stood in the middle of the study, stunned.

A moment later Carter's mother came downstairs and into the study. "Carter?" she said. "Did I hear your father's car pull out?"

Carter nodded. "He said he had an errand to do."

"That's funny," Mrs. Phillips said, shrugging slightly. She seemed to focus on her daughter's face now. "And what are you doing, just standing in the middle of the room with that strange expression? Has something happened?"

"Well, yes. Daddy called the testing service to find out what my math score was."

"And?"

"It's seven hundred thirty."

Mrs. Phillips crossed the room and hugged Carter. "That's wonderful, dear! Your father must be so happy. Isn't it wonderful?"

"It's great."

"Carter, we should celebrate! Why don't you look happier about this? You look sort of numb."

Carter gave her mother a kiss and said, "It just hasn't sunk in yet, that's all. I can't believe it's really true."

"Well, it *is* true. It's terrific news." She pulled away from Carter now and started poking through her purse.

"I wish I could stay and celebrate with you," she said. "But I've got to run out and look at flower arrangements for the Spring Fling." She gave Carter a kiss and added, "See you at dinner, dear."

Mrs. Phillips left. Carter wandered into the hallway, not sure what to do with herself. She sat down on the bottom step of the carpeted staircase.

It worked, she thought. The whole plan worked out perfectly. I got what I wanted. Nothing bad happened.

So why don't I feel happy?

She had no idea how much time had passed before she heard her father's Mercedes pull into the driveway. A minute later he came into the house, all smiles.

In his hand he held a tiny package, wrapped in robin's egg blue paper and tied with a thin white ribbon.

He held the package out to Carter, who was still sitting on the stairs. She looked at him in surprise.

"This is for you, Carter," said Judge Phillips. "To celebrate the fruits of all your hard work."

He gave her the package, then kissed her on the forehead. "I'm so proud of you."

Carter opened the package. Inside was a pair of sparkling diamond earrings.

Her stomach dropped to the floor. They were beautiful. No, they were gorgeous. But she knew she didn't deserve them. She couldn't help but think of what she had done to get those earrings.

Cheater. Cheater.

The word repeated in her mind.

She tried to smile brightly at her father, hiding her guilty feelings. "Daddy," she said, "they're beautiful. Really beautiful. You shouldn't have done this."

"Put them on, Carter," said her father. "I want to see how they look."

Dutifully she put on the earrings. Her father beamed and kissed her again.

"Brilliant diamonds for a brilliant girl. Now, I have some work to do in my study, but I'll see you at dinner."

Still grinning, he went into his study and closed the door.

Carter stood and made her way upstairs to her bedroom. She stood before her dresser, staring at herself in the mirror. The diamond earrings seemed to give off a glare. She cringed.

Her father's words echoed through her mind. "Brilliant diamonds for a brilliant girl."

I'm not a brilliant girl, she thought. I'm a cheater. And Daddy must never find out.

Dan met Carter at her locker after school the next day. Carter knew she had to talk to him—to break their date for Friday night—but she dreaded doing it. Worse, she had no idea what to say. She had avoided Dan all day. Now he'd finally caught up with her.

"Want to go to the mall?" he asked her. "Just hang out, look around."

"Sure," said Carter. At least the mall would provide some distractions. "Let's go."

They strolled past the stores on the second tier of the Division Street Mall, sipping Cokes and window-shopping.

"Hey," said Dan. "Have you heard anything about your math test yet?"

Carter nodded. "Dad called early, of course."

"So? How'd you do?"

She tried to smile. "I did great—seven thirty."

Dan's face lit up. "Great? That's fantastic! Way to go, Carter. I know that really meant a lot to you. *And* to your dad."

"It did. Look what Daddy bought me as soon as he found out." She tucked her hair behind her right ear to show him one diamond earring.

Dan whistled. "Wow. He really *was* happy, wasn't he?"

Carter laughed, just a little.

"You see," Dan went on. "You didn't need me to take the test for you, after all. You did great all by yourself."

Carter smiled weakly.

Dan stopped in front of a jewelry store window. There were gold rings, bracelets, and necklaces laid out on black velvet. He stood for a few minutes with his hands in his pockets, admiring the display.

Carter was restless. The last thing she felt like doing just then was to stare at jewelry.

Dan continued to stand there and pointed to a row of necklaces. "If you could have any one of those necklaces, which would you pick?"

Carter sighed. She wasn't in the mood to play "which would you pick" just then. But to make him happy, she pointed to a gold locket in the middle of the display.

"That one," she said and walked on.

He followed her. "You know," he said, "we should celebrate tomorrow night. Let's do something really special."

Carter raised her face to him now with a pained expression. Here it comes, she thought.

"Oh, Dan," she said. "I almost forgot. We had a date for tomorrow night, didn't we?"

She hated to lie to him. But just once more, she had to do it. She had to.

"What do you mean, you almost forgot? Of course we have a date tomorrow."

"Dan, I'm sorry. I know I promised you we'd go out tomorrow, but Daddy wants to take me and Mother out to dinner to celebrate. And tomorrow's the only night he can do it. He's so busy right now with the trial and everything. . . ."

She glanced reluctantly at Dan to see how he was taking this. He was frowning.

"Dan, please understand. I know I had to break a date with you last weekend, but this is the last time, I promise. We can go out Saturday night if you want—"

"I can't go out Saturday night. My grandparents are coming over."

"Oh." Carter focused on the rust-colored tile floor. "What about during the day? We could meet at the club."

"Okay. We'll play tennis on Saturday," he said unhappily.

Carter felt terrible. "I'm really sorry, Dan," she said again. She couldn't stop apologizing.

"Don't worry, Carter. I understand. It's okay."

But for the rest of the afternoon, he acted distant. Carter was afraid that it *wasn't* okay.

She met Adam on the corner of Village and Mission Friday night, dressed, as the last time, in jeans. He came by in his Mustang and drove her to the movies.

They watched a horror movie, a silly one that

42

was more funny than scary, since the gory effects were so obviously fake. After the lights went down, Adam put his arm around Carter's shoulders. She didn't make him take his arm away.

When the movie ended, Adam and Carter found the Mustang in the parking lot and got in. Adam pulled out without saying where he was going.

Carter had assumed he was taking her home. But she soon knew they weren't driving in the direction of North Hills.

"Where are we going?" she asked.

Adam just said, "No place special."

He turned down Fear Street. Carter remembered that Adam lived on Fear Street.

She stared out the window at the dark trees that lined the road. Huge, ramshackle old Victorian houses surrounded a few smaller, newer houses—run-down little boxes. Adam pulled the car into a driveway next to one of these.

It was a one-story house with a rickety porch stuck on the front. Except for a yellow bulb by the side door, the house was completely dark.

"Well," Adam said with a hint of sarcasm, "here we are. Home sweet home."

He pulled the keys from the ignition and started to get out of the car.

Carter made no move to follow.

It was obvious to her that no one was home. She wasn't sure she wanted to be so completely alone with Adam.

On the other hand, she was curious to see what

his house was like. And she couldn't forget that kiss—that kiss he had given her a week before.

Would he kiss her again?

Half of her was afraid he would—and the other half longed for it to happen again.

He closed the car door and headed to the house. He didn't look back. He seemed to know that she'd follow him. And she did.

He unlocked the side door and flicked on the light. Carter found herself in a tidy kitchen.

"We've got the place to ourselves," Adam said. "Mom works nights."

He opened the refrigerator, grabbed a couple of sodas, and led her to the couch in the living room. He turned on a lamp and sat beside her.

The living room was neat, but shabby. The furniture—a worn couch, a rag carpet, some scuffed wooden chairs, and a coffee table covered with white cup rings—reminded Carter of the furniture she'd made fun of in a mountain cabin her family had rented once.

"So," said Adam, flipping open his can of soda. "Did you get your test score yet?"

"It was great—seven thirty. Thanks for doing such a good job, Adam."

"No problem." He took a swig of soda, then put the can on the table and turned toward her. He touched her hair, then her earlobe.

"Nice earrings," he said. "Are they new?"

Carter's hands flew to her ears. She'd meant to

take the diamond earrings off before this date, but she'd forgotten. She felt embarrassed to be wearing such extravagant jewelry in a modest house like Adam's.

"Daddy gave them to me," she said, blushing.

"After he heard your test score, right?"

He fingered her earlobe, watching the diamond sparkle in the light. It seemed to fascinate him.

Carter pulled her head away. "Let's not talk about the test," she said. "That's all over now."

"All right. I'll change the subject. Let's talk about your friend Jill."

"What about her?"

"She's cool. You know my friend Ray Owens? Ray really likes her."

"So?" Ray Owens had five tattoos and three earrings. Unlike Adam, he wasn't smart. As far as Carter was concerned, Jill and Ray lived on two different planets.

"So I want you to fix them up. We'll double— you, me, Ray, and Jill. Tomorrow night."

Carter gaped at him. Not only was he demanding another date with her, now he wanted to drag Jill into it too.

Jill would never go along with it. How could Carter explain it to her?

Still, Carter was careful when she answered him. Diplomatic.

"Jill's already got a boyfriend. She's really not free to go out with other people."

45

"That's not important," Adam said. "Ray's my friend. He wants to go out with Jill. You're going to set it up. No problem, right?"

She started to protest, but he stopped her by pressing his mouth against hers.

She melted. It was a great kiss. But then he pressed down on her harder. She tried to get up. He wouldn't let her. His chin brushed roughly against her cheek.

"Stop!" she screamed. "Stop!" She jumped up, started to back away.

He followed her, grinning, and pressed her against the wall.

chapter

6

Carter struggled, trying to get away from him, trying to breathe. But he held her hard against the wall. She gave one big push against his chest.

He smiled at her arrogantly. She was pinned. He had complete control of the situation. They both knew it.

Then all at once he let her go.

She moved away quickly and straightened her shirt. "Whoa. Look, Adam," she said angrily. "You took the test for me. I appreciate it. We agreed that I'd go out with you—once. This is already our second date. I have a boyfriend. I've done more than I had to. Now you've got to leave me alone."

Adam's eyes burned with anger. He began to pace the room.

Carter felt a stab of fear. His eyes were cold with pent-up anger. He seemed capable of anything.

"What's your problem, Carter?" he sneered, turning on her. "Aren't you having a good time?"

She was really afraid of him now, afraid of doing something that might let that fury loose.

"Listen," she said, "if I set up this double date, will you leave me alone?"

She could almost see the anger in his eyes fade. It had worked. His cool demeanor returned.

"It's worth a shot, Carter. You won't know until you try."

She stood still for a minute. She didn't know what to do next.

"Go on," he told her. "Call Jill now."

He pointed toward a table in the hallway, next to the kitchen. The phone sat on the table.

Carter walked stiffly to the table and picked up the receiver. With a glance at Adam, she dialed Jill's number.

Please don't be home, Jill, Carter prayed. If Jill wasn't home, then maybe she wouldn't have to do what Adam asked.

But Jill answered the phone.

"Hi, Jill. It's me."

"Hi, Carter. Is something wrong?"

"Wrong? Why do you ask that?"

"Well, you're calling kind of late."

Carter had no idea what time it was. She glanced at her watch. It was after eleven.

"Sorry, Jill. I didn't mean to call so late. Maybe I'd better call you back tomorrow."

Carter glanced at Adam. He was sitting on the arm of the couch, watching her. At her last words, he shook his head firmly.

"No, it's okay. Gary and I are just hanging out," Jill said. "What's up?"

"Well, Jill," she began, trying to sound cheerful, "Adam Messner asked if you and I would like to double tomorrow night."

"Double? You mean, you and Adam with me and Gary?"

"Um, no, not with Gary. With Ray Owens."

"What?"

"It might be fun, don't you think?" Carter bluffed.

"Hold on a minute, Carter." She heard Jill put down the phone and tell Gary she was taking the call upstairs. When Jill picked up the extension, Gary hung up the downstairs phone.

Jill spoke in a hushed voice. "Carter, what's this all about? Adam and Ray? What about Dan? What about Gary?"

Carter twisted the phone cord nervously around her finger. She was in a tight spot. She didn't want to say anything to Jill that would make her suspicious. And she couldn't say anything that would make Adam angry.

"It's just a date, Jill. It's not as if we're going to elope with them or anything."

"I don't get it, Carter. Why would you want to do this?"

"Just for fun," Carter said brightly. She let go of the cord and started playing with the handle of the drawer in the phone table.

"Fun? You think going out with losers is fun?"

"Don't say that, Jill. I mean, how well do you really know them? You're prejudiced."

"I am not. I'm very open-minded."

"Well, if you're so open-minded, you'll give it a shot. Come on, Jill. As a favor?"

Jill sighed. "I don't believe this. All right, Carter. Since I happen to be free tomorrow night, I'll go out with you and Adam and Ray. But I want you to know that I'm doing this for one reason, and one reason only: something's going on with you and Adam, and I'm going to find out what it is."

Adam came up behind Carter. She turned toward him and gave him a nervous grin. "Great, great. I'm looking forward to it too, Jill. See you tomorrow night."

She hung up the phone, still fiddling with the drawer. Absently, she pulled it open.

Adam stood behind her, peering over her shoulder as she glanced into the drawer.

Something gleamed among the scraps of paper and pencils and tape in the drawer. Something shiny and black.

A gun.

Adam reached around her and picked up the pistol. She stared at him in shock.

"Like it?" he asked her.

She was shaking now. She was alone in a house on Fear Street with a guy who had a gun.

"Is it yours?"

He nodded. "You never know when you might need a gun, Carter. Who knows, even *you* might need one someday. Want to hold it?"

He pushed the muzzle against her.

She gasped and pushed the gun away. "Are you threatening me?"

"I don't need a gun to threaten you, Carter." He was grinning smugly.

Shaking, she ran into the kitchen.

Adam didn't try to stop her. His laughter followed her, though, loud and cruel.

A few seconds later she was out the door and running down the street as fast as she could. She didn't think about where she was going. She just ran.

Fear Street. Dim yellow light fell on the street sign. Carter ran past the sign, her heart thudding.

Got to get away. Got to get away from here!

She saw a bus pull up to the curb. She jumped on. With a wheeze, the bus doors closed and it pulled away.

She stumbled to a seat in the back of the bus, panting. She pressed her face against the window, watching for Adam.

No. He hadn't followed.

It was late, so the bus made very few stops. The only other passengers were two old men and a middle-aged woman in a flowered dress.

The bus wound its way through Shadyside toward North Hills. Trying to calm herself, Carter watched the town go by outside her window. The streetlights cast empty pools of yellow on the asphalt, which darkened as the bus passed them by.

Up Park Drive. Carter got off a couple blocks from her house. She started for home.

The street stretched dark, quiet, empty.

Empty, except for the slow approach of a car behind her.

First, she heard the hum of the car's engine. Then she saw the headlights illuminate the sidewalk.

She waited for the car to pass her. But it didn't. It inched along, a few yards behind her, as if it were following her.

Carter turned to look. The headlights glared in her face.

She couldn't see anything. She shielded her eyes from the light.

She turned and started walking more quickly.

The car kept a steady pace behind her.

What's going on? she wondered, frightened. Is it Adam?

She tried to see who it was again. The lights were too bright.

She began to jog. What's going on? Why is he *doing* this? She began to run. The car still followed.

It stayed right behind her, its headlights focused on her like a spotlight as she ran.

*F*inally she was fumbling for the keys on the front porch of her house, then she was darting into the safety of the front hall. She slammed the door and leaned against it for a long while, waiting to catch her breath.

She worked up the courage to peek through the side window.

Was the car still there?

Yes. There it was, in front of her house. Its headlights still on.

Who is it? She still couldn't see the make of the car.

Carter continued to peer out the window, frozen.

What do they want? Why was that car following me?

A moment later the car peeled out with a squeal of tires.

Carter hurried up to her room, her entire body trembling. Her parents were in bed.

Carter usually turned off the hall light outside her bedroom. But she decided to leave it on. It made her feel a little safer.

Who was in that car? It had to be Adam, she thought. The bus had taken such an indirect route to North Hills. Adam could easily have beaten her home.

Then she remembered what had happened the first time she came home from a date with Adam: Sheila had been waiting for her.

Could it have been Sheila in the car?

Carter undressed and got into bed, still trembling. If only she could have seen what kind of car it was. It could have been a Mustang, she thought. It could have been Adam's Mustang.

I just don't know. . . .

The next day she went to the club at eleven to meet Dan. She went into the locker room and changed. When she came out, she found Dan waiting for her at the snack bar.

He was sitting at one of the white wicker tables, which was covered with magazines and catalogs of sports equipment. To her surprise, he hadn't changed into his tennis clothes—he was still wearing jeans and a blue oxford shirt.

She walked over to kiss him, expecting him to smile at her as usual. He didn't smile, and he didn't kiss her back.

She sat across the table from him. "Why aren't you dressed?"

He ignored her question. "What's going on, Carter?" he asked quietly. "Are you dumping me?"

Carter was shocked. Where had this come from?

"Dumping you?" she said. "Of course not! Why are you asking me that?"

He didn't answer her directly. Instead he asked her, "What did you do last night?"

Her stomach knotted up. What did he know? "I went out with my parents," she lied. "Just like I told you."

"I heard you went to the movies with Adam Messner."

She tried her best to act outraged. "That's ridiculous. Who told you that?"

"Ryan Dalton said he saw you there. At some horror movie. He was sitting three rows behind you."

"He made a mistake. I didn't go to the movies last night. I went out to dinner with my parents. I swear I did!"

Dan just looked at her.

"He must have seen another girl who looked like me," said Carter. "Ryan doesn't even know me. And besides, Dan, why would *I* go out with Adam Messner?"

She went to him and put her arms around him, to reassure him. He stiffened when she touched him and made no move to hug her back.

I can't believe this is happening, she thought. Why did Ryan Dalton have to be at the movies last night?

She held him tighter, willing him to believe her. At last Dan's expression did relax a little.

He wants to believe me, she thought. All I have to do is distract him. I've got to change the subject.

She reached across the table and picked up a thick boating catalog. She started flipping through the glossy pages.

"Hey, Dan," she said, trying to sound cheerful. "If you could have any one of these sailboats, which would you pick?"

She passed the catalog to him and smiled.

He smiled back at her, a weak smile.

It's working, she thought. I've convinced him that everything's okay. This game makes him feel as if everything is back to normal.

He picked a graceful wooden sloop.

"Maybe we'll go on a cruise together someday," Carter said. "We'll get a boat like this and sail from island to island, just the two of us."

Dan said, "Someday. Maybe."

"Come on, let's play tennis," said Carter. "Go get dressed. I'll meet you on the courts."

Dan went into the men's locker room to change. Carter picked up her tennis racquet and walked down to the courts to practice her serve while she waited for him.

When Dan arrived, they played an easy match. By the end Carter felt fairly sure that things were okay between them. When they parted at the locker rooms, he gave her a kiss and a smile.

"Have fun with your grandparents tonight," she called.

He rolled his eyes and waved goodbye.

The women's locker room was empty. Carter opened her locker and pulled out her tennis bag.

She heard the locker room door open and rapid footsteps move toward her. She looked up. It was Jill.

"Hi," said Carter, smiling.

"Hi," said Jill. She didn't smile back. "I'm glad you're here. I was hoping to talk to you before we get together tonight."

Carter suppressed a sigh. The date tonight. She wasn't looking forward to it—especially after her scare last night and Dan's accusation that morning. Also, she hated to drag Jill into the whole thing.

But what could she do?

The more she knew of Adam, the more ruthless he seemed to her. She knew he would tell her father that she'd cheated on the math test if she didn't cooperate with him. She had to keep Adam from telling. She'd do almost anything.

"Come on, Carter," Jill said. "Tell me the real reason why we're going on this double date tonight."

"About that date," Carter said in a low voice. "Listen, Jill, promise me you won't tell anyone about it—especially Dan. It's no big deal, and I don't want him to get the wrong idea."

"The wrong idea! You're going out with another guy! How could he misunderstand *that?*"

"Jill, I can't explain it to you now. But there is a reason we're going on this date tonight, and it's not because I'm crazy about Adam or anything like that. Please, just don't ask any more questions. We'll go out and that will be that. Okay?"

Jill frowned, confused, but she didn't argue. She grabbed a towel and padded into the shower.

Carter sighed. Things were getting more and more complicated. Maybe after tonight, she thought hopefully, it will all simmer down.

She reached into her tennis bag for her hairbrush.

And froze.

Her hand had grabbed something strange— something warm and sticky. She pulled her hand out of the bag.

She screamed.

Her hand was covered with blood.

chapter

8

"Ohh!"

Carter uttered a shrill cry as she stared at her bloody hand, horrified.

What *happened?*

After a moment she made herself peer into the tennis bag.

She couldn't see anything.

She shoved her hand back into the bag. There was that awful, warm stickiness. She shuddered.

And pulled out a large, slimy, bloody thing.

A heart!

A human heart?

No.

It wasn't the right size to have come from a person. Too big.

She dropped it and gagged as it made a loud *splat* on the floor. She closed her eyes.

It's an animal's heart, Carter thought, her stom-

59

ach tightening with disgust. It must have come from a cow, or some other large animal.

Glancing down reluctantly, she spied a sticky piece of paper stuck to the heart with a pin.

She bent down quickly and pulled the paper off with a sharp tug.

On the paper, scrawled in blood, was a message: "Careful—or you'll break Daddy's heart."

With a jolt, she let the paper drop to the floor.

Adam! How could he do such a horrible thing!

Carter's entire body shuddered in disgust.

Jill came running out of the shower, her hair full of suds, wrapping a towel around her. "What's wrong? I thought I heard a scream!"

She took one look at Carter's bloody hand and gasped. She ran to Carter to help her. Carter quickly kicked the heart under a bench to hide it from Jill.

"Carter, what happened?"

Carter was still shaking and she couldn't hide it. "It—it's nothing, really," she said, trying to steady her voice. "I mean, it looks much worse than it is. I—I cut my hand. On my razor. I was reaching into my bag to get it, and the cover must have fallen off. I slit one of my fingers—"

"Oh, my gosh," said Jill. "Let me see it."

Carter stepped away from her quickly. "No, no—it'll be okay."

She went to a sink and started washing her hands. "I'll just run some water over it, and put a Band-Aid on it and it'll be fine."

"But there's so much blood!"

"Really, it's not as bad as it looks. You'd better get back in the shower and rinse the soap out of your hair."

Jill stood in a soapy puddle, staring at her friend with her mouth open.

"Go on, Jill. It's just a tiny cut."

"Well, if you're sure you're all right—"

"I'm fine, I swear."

Jill hurried back to the shower. Carter dried her hands and finished changing.

How could Adam be so cruel? she thought angrily. And how did he get that thing in my bag?

Another thought pushed its way to the surface, but Carter tried to hold it down.

It wouldn't stay down, though. The thought returned, taunting her.

How can you see him tonight, after all that's happened?

After all he's done to you—the gun, and following you in his car, and now this gross joke—how can you go out on a date with him, and fix up your best friend with that horrible Ray, and pretend that you like them?

She knew why she was doing it. But she didn't want to think about it.

On her way out of the club, she threw her tennis bag—with the heart in it—into the trash bin.

* * *

Jill drove over to Carter's house that evening. They took Carter's car to meet the guys. They wanted to go together.

They drove into the Old Village to a club called Benny's. Adam had told Carter how to get there.

Carter saw Adam's black Mustang parked on the street in front of Benny's so she knew he and Ray were already inside. She spotted a red neon sign over a basement window—BENNY's.

There was a flyer in the window, advertising the band playing that night. It was called the Grimes. Carter and Jill could hear a crash of drums floating up out of the dive.

The girls glanced at each other nervously. Then they started down the stairs to the basement club.

Benny's was run-down with a cement floor, peeling plaster walls, and dim lighting. In the front stood a cluster of chairs and wooden tables covered with scratches and graffiti. In the middle of the long room stood a pool table and against the wall, a bar. In the back was an open space where the band played. The bar was decorated with green streamers and leprechauns for Saint Patrick's Day.

Carter scanned the room for Adam. The place seemed to be full of long-haired guys in jeans and T-shirts. Carter saw only three other girls.

"I see them," said Jill. She pointed to a round table. Adam and Ray were sitting there, staring at Carter and Jill. They seemed to be waiting to see how long it would take the girls to find them.

62

Carter plastered a stiff smile on her face and sat down at the table.

"Hi, Adam," she said. "You know my friend Jill. Jill, do you know Ray Owens?"

"Hi, Ray," Jill said politely.

"Jill. Hey. Looking good," said Ray. He was wearing a black T-shirt with a hole under one arm and a dirty pair of black jeans. There were three silver studs in his left ear—one in the shape of a skull—and Carter could see two of his five tattoos on a forearm. A blue mermaid and a red heart with "Harley" written inside it. By the greasiness of his hair, Carter guessed he hadn't washed it in a week.

Jill gave Carter a wide, nervous smile. Carter knew what she was trying to say. The smile meant, "What have you gotten me into?"

The throbbing noise suddenly stopped as the band went on a break. Adam put his arm over Carter's chair and grinned at her. She didn't smile back at him, but she let his arm stay where it was.

Now Ray pulled Jill's chair—with Jill in it—toward him. "Come on, don't be a stranger," he said.

Jill leaned away from Ray, but he just moved in closer.

Two guys in motorcycle jackets leaned over their table. "Hey, Adam, Ray," they said.

Ray reached across the table and slapped the hand of the taller guy. "Yo, Curt, how's it going?"

"Where'd these babes come from?" asked the

other guy, whose name was Manny. He looked the girls over and murmured, "Not bad."

"They're North Hills girls," said Adam. He squeezed Carter's shoulder and added, "They're out slumming tonight."

Manny and Curt exchanged knowing looks. Carter felt like sliding under the table.

"Why don't you guys sit down?" said Ray. "Pull up some chairs."

"We're out of here," said Curt. "You going to Eddie's tonight?"

"We might stop by, after we leave here," said Adam.

"See you there, then," said Curt. "And bring the babes."

Curt and Manny left. The band started up again. While they played, it was too noisy to talk. Ray tugged on Jill's arm and screamed, "Let's dance."

He pulled her toward the back of the room. Jill glanced back at Carter.

Carter watched them on the dance floor. Ray shut his eyes and danced with abandon, slamming into Jill once in a while. Jill was swaying from side to side, halfheartedly. She seemed very uncomfortable.

Adam put his mouth to Carter's ear and shouted, "Don't they make a nice couple?"

She checked his expression to see just how he meant this. He was sneering. She should have known.

The song ended, and Jill started to leave the

dance floor. But Ray grabbed her by the arm and pulled her back. He held her tightly against him. The music was loud and fast, but Ray ignored the beat and slow-danced.

Jill struggled to get out of his arms. Carter watched with growing concern as Ray gripped Jill even tighter. He wouldn't let her get away.

A few of the guys on the dance floor watched him, laughing. No one did anything to help Jill.

Adam was watching too. He started to laugh.

This made Carter furious. Ray was a beast—and Adam thought it was funny!

Jill was trying harder to get away now. She tried to hit Ray, but he pinned her arms to her sides.

"Adam!" Carter shouted. "Go over and stop him!"

Adam shrugged and said, "Hey, it's none of my business."

That was it. Carter couldn't sit on the sidelines and watch anymore. If Adam wouldn't help Jill, Carter would. After all, Carter was responsible for getting Jill into this mess.

She jumped up, furious, and stormed onto the dance floor. "Let her go!" she screamed at Ray.

Jill was crying. But Ray's eyes were closed, and he was grinning. That made Carter even angrier.

Carter tried to pry Ray's arms from around Jill's waist. Everyone who'd been dancing stopped to watch.

Ray wouldn't let go. Jill was hysterical. Carter was trying to break them apart, and everybody else was just laughing. The more Carter tried to help Jill, the harder the guys laughed.

Five guys formed a circle around Carter, Jill, and Ray. They moved in closer. Ray let go of Jill at last, but the other guys grabbed her and Carter.

"Get your hands *off* me!" Carter shouted.

She struggled to get away. More guys moved in.

The band stopped playing, put down their instruments, and joined the group. Carter didn't see any other girls anywhere now.

Her only hope was Adam—and Carter knew he was a faint hope.

She saw him sitting alone at their table. She glared at him.

He got up from the table and moved toward the crowd.

He's not so terrible, Carter thought. He's going to help us.

Adam stood outside the circle of guys and said, "Hey, be careful with those girls."

Carter felt the grip on her arms loosen. These guys respected Adam. They're going to let us go, she thought with relief.

But then Adam smiled and added, "They're from North Hills, you know. If you wrinkle their clothes, their daddies will sue you!"

The room broke into laughter. Carter's jaw dropped. How could he? He was spurring these creeps on!

She glanced at Jill, who was crying so hard she

could barely struggle anymore. Two guys held her by the arms.

Carter began to panic.

We've got to get out of here, she thought. We've got to get away, before something terrible happens.

She was afraid to think beyond that, to think of what exactly she was afraid of.

Adam moved in front of Carter and took her face in his hands. "Carter's daddy is a judge," he told the crowd. "She'll do *anything* to make him happy. Won't you, Carter?"

Her face burned with anger and shame, and hot tears sprang to her eyes. "I hate you, Adam," she said. "I hate you!" But she knew that nothing she said to Adam could hurt him. And she knew he would say whatever he wanted to her.

Ray leaned his head down to kiss Jill, while one of his friends taunted her. "What does *your* daddy do, rich girl?"

The taunts and ugly remarks grew louder. The laughing stopped.

Carter saw that Adam, Ray, and all the guys around them had hard looks on their faces.

No one held Carter now, but she couldn't get away. She was surrounded by a tight circle of leering guys.

Someone shoved her up against Jill. She and Jill clung to each other for support, as the circle of guys closed in on them.

Jill's face was wet and red. Her lips were trembling, and she was shaking uncontrollably. Carter hugged her protectively.

"Let us go!" Carter cried. She tried to act brave, as if she weren't afraid of them. "Let us go! I'm warning you!"

The guys ignored her plea. They moved in closer. Their expressions were hard and terrifying.

Ray leered at Carter, his earrings gleaming in the dim light. Carter felt his hot breath on her face.

"What's your hurry, girls?" he said. "It's early. The party's just getting started."

C arter screamed.

She kicked out with all her might.

Jill thrashed her arms wildly, trying to clear an escape route.

Someone came up behind Carter and grabbed her arms. She leaned against him and kicked Ray in the chest. He fell backward against two other guys, knocking them down. One guy's head hit the table with a crack.

The other guy climbed to his feet and angrily shoved Ray. Carter and Jill struggled to get away. But they were trapped in the middle of the angry shoving match.

Carter cried out as Adam punched somebody in the jaw. Someone else kicked a table over.

Soon everybody in the place was caught up in fighting. Carter grabbed Jill and pulled her out of the middle of the brawl.

"Come on—run!" Carter cried.

She pulled Jill by the hand, and they ran blindly out of Benny's, out onto the street.

Carter didn't stop until she reached her car. Panting loudly, they both threw themselves into the car, slammed the doors, and locked them.

Shaking, Carter fumbled the key into the ignition. Then she threw the car into Drive and roared off, the tires squealing.

Leaning over the wheel, Carter didn't stop until she came to a red light at the edge of the Old Village. She glanced frantically into her rearview mirror.

No one.

No one was following them. They were safe.

Jill was slumped back in the seat beside her, crying and shaking. Carter said nothing. First, she wanted to get safely home.

She sped up into North Hills. A few minutes later she pulled into her driveway and helped Jill into the house.

Her parents were in bed. Carter took Jill into the kitchen. She sat her in a chair and put her arms around her shoulders.

"Ssshhh," said Carter, trying to soothe her friend. "Jill, I'm so sorry, I'm so sorry. . . ."

Jill cried for a few minutes longer. Then she stopped and wiped her eyes. Carter brought her some tissues and a glass of water.

Jill drank the water and grew calmer, though her eyes still were red rimmed. "Carter," she said, "what were we doing with those guys?"

Carter stared at the floor. She couldn't meet Jill's eye.

"Carter—" Jill insisted.

"I'm really, really sorry, Jill," she said. "I never thought it would turn out so badly. I had no idea . . ."

Her voice trailed off. What could she say? She was so ashamed. She had put her friend in danger.

I should have known it would be dangerous, she thought. Adam has a gun. He's blackmailing me. He doesn't care what happens to me. And he's capable of anything. I know that now.

But how could she tell Jill the truth—that Adam had threatened to reveal Carter as a cheater if she didn't do what he wanted?

Jill would never forgive her for using her this way. And why should she? Carter knew that *she* would be furious if Jill had done the same thing to her.

"Carter, I still don't understand," Jill said. "I know there's some reason why you wanted me to go out with Ray. I know that there's something between you and Adam. What is it? You owe me an explanation."

Carter knew she was right—she owed Jill an explanation. But Jill wouldn't get one—not the real one, anyway.

"Jill, I'm really sorry. I—I lost a bet with Adam. This date was the price I had to pay. I should never have gotten you involved—"

"What bet?" Jill asked.

What bet?

"It's so silly I'm afraid to tell you," Carter lied. Then she thought of something.

"I bet him he couldn't beat Richard in the tennis match last weekend," she said. "I thought it was a sure thing—you can understand why."

She glanced at Jill. Was Jill buying it? It was hard to tell.

"The important thing is that I had to follow through with it," Carter went on. "The date, I mean. And I was afraid to go by myself. That's why I wanted you to come with me. Jill, will you ever forgive me? I promise, nothing like this will ever happen again!"

Jill put an arm around her friend. "I know you didn't mean for all that to happen," she said. "You were in as much danger in that horrible club as I was. Of course I'll forgive you."

The two girls sat quietly in the kitchen, hugging each other. Carter heard the refrigerator click and start to hum. She held her friend tighter. It scared her to think how close they had come to disaster that night. It terrified her to think that she had almost gotten her best friend hurt.

Adam, she thought angrily. He's taking this thing too far—*way* too far.

She was furious at him. But she was even more furious with herself for letting him control her so completely. Whatever he had asked, she had done.

But no longer.

That's it, she thought. The end. No more black-mail. I've had enough.

Jill stood up to get another glass of water. "I feel better now," she said. "I think I'm ready to go home."

Carter walked Jill to her car, which was parked in front of the house. She apologized again, over and over.

At last Jill said, "Stop apologizing, Carter. I know you're sorry. I know you didn't mean for anything bad to happen. So let's forget about it."

Carter smiled and nodded. Jill was being so nice about the whole thing. It only made Carter feel worse.

Carter waved as Jill drove off. Then she went back into the house.

She rinsed Jill's glass and put it in the dishwasher. Abruptly the phone rang.

Carter glanced at the clock. It was after midnight. Could it be some kind of emergency for her father?

She picked up the receiver. "Hello?"

A high-pitched voice whispered, "You were with Adam tonight, weren't you? Weren't you?"

It was Sheila.

Carter was too stunned to speak.

Sheila said, "You don't have to answer me, 'cause I know the truth. I know what's going on between you two."

"Sheila, nothing's—"

73

"Don't lie to me, Carter! I know you're a big liar. I don't even want to hear what you have to say. You just listen to me.

"Adam can't keep any secrets from me. I know everything he does. And I'll find a way to keep you and Adam apart—*for good.*"

chapter

10

"So, how'd it go with your grandparents on Saturday?"

Dan and Carter were walking down the hall at Shadyside High Monday afternoon, on their way to advanced math class. Carter was dreading it.

Dan smiled. "It was nice. Boring, but nice. It was my grandmother's birthday. She's seventy."

"Seventy. Wow."

"What did *you* do on Saturday night?"

Carter swallowed hard. "Me? Oh, I was with Jill."

She didn't have time to say more than that, to her relief. They had reached their classroom.

Dan and Carter went in. Dan sat next to Carter, and Carter sat next to Jill. Adam wasn't in his seat.

Jill gave her a funny sort of smile. Carter gave her one back.

Mr. Raub closed the classroom door. A second later it opened again. Both Jill and Carter looked up. Carter saw the dread she was feeling reflected in Jill's face.

It was Adam. Last one in, as usual.

He cast a smug glance toward Carter and Jill. Both girls quickly turned away. Adam loped to his seat in the back of the room.

Carter felt Dan's eyes on her. Had he caught Adam's glance? Did he wonder what it meant?

When class was over, Carter let Dan and Jill go on ahead of her. She walked slowly down the hall, sure that Adam would approach her.

He did.

She felt a tap on her shoulder and turned to face him. He opened his mouth to speak, but she spoke first.

"Adam, I've had enough," she said in a low voice. "Our little arrangement is over. From now on, you're going to leave me alone. Do you understand?"

Then, nervously, she waited for his reaction. Would he burst into a violent rage? Would he walk away?

He stayed calm and didn't look the least bit rattled.

"You're right about one thing, Carter," he said. "Things just aren't working out between us, are they? We do need to change our 'relationship.'"

Carter didn't know what to say. Why was he acting so agreeable? What was he up to?

"I've been thinking it over, Carter," he went on. "And I don't think we should go out again."

She was too wary to feel relieved. This was what she wanted—but there had to be a catch.

"I'm glad we agree," she said carefully.

"You know, the little service I performed for you—I think we both know what I'm talking about. It was pretty valuable, right? I mean, most people would pay a lot of money for it. Yet you got this valuable service for free. That's not fair, is it?"

She said nothing.

"I figure taking an important test like that—and getting good results—it must be worth at least a thousand dollars."

So that was it. He wanted money.

She couldn't believe it. She was angry now, and she let him know it.

"Listen," Carter said, trying not to speak too loudly. "You offered to take that test for me. You told me that all I'd have to do was go out with you once. I've done much more than that now—*much* more. But no matter what I do, it's not enough. How much longer is this going on?"

Adam casually studied the lines in his right hand. "It can stop whenever you want, Carter," he said. "Of course, I'll have to tell your father everything. . . ."

Carter's muscles tensed.

He had complete power over her. If she didn't do what he wanted, he could ruin her life.

"Look," she said angrily, "I'll give you the money if you promise to leave me alone!"

"That might work," he said. "Give it a try."

He walked away slowly, casually. She stared after him, burning with anger and frustration.

Where would she get a thousand dollars? she wondered glumly as she walked to her locker.

She pulled open her locker door and glanced into the mirror inside. There was a flash, then a sparkle.

That was it.

She touched a hand to her left ear. The diamond earrings. She'd have to sell them. She had no choice.

She took the earrings off and put them in an envelope. If only she had the box with her . . . But this would have to do.

After school she took a bus to the Old Village. There were some antique shops there. Carter remembered going once with her mother. Mrs. Phillips's stepmother had died and left her some jewelry, most of it "not to my taste," as Carter's mother had put it. She'd taken the jewelry to a shop on Antique Row and sold it.

Now Carter clutched the diamond earrings her father had given her and scanned the four antique shops in front of her. She tried to remember which one she'd gone to with her mother. That was the one she *didn't* want to go to now. She didn't want to take any chances that her parents would find out. And she didn't want anyone to recognize her.

Bentley's was the shop her mother had gone to. Carter chose the one farthest away from it. It was called Corelli's Antiques.

A little bell rang as she pushed the door open. A tall old man stood leaning over a glass counter. Behind him Carter saw a wall full of antique clocks, all set to the correct time and ticking and whirring noisily.

Carter approached the glass counter.

"Hello, miss," said the old man, straightening up and smiling. He had a slight Italian accent. "How may I help you?"

Carter opened the envelope and let the diamond earrings fall into her palm. She held them out to the old man.

"Someone gave me these earrings," she said. "But I already have a pair like them. I was wondering how much I could get for them."

The old man studied her face. Does he suspect something? Carter wondered. Maybe he thinks I stole them.

She glanced away, pretending to be fascinated by a marble statue of an angel. When she turned back to the man, he was examining the earrings through a jeweler's loupe.

"These earrings are of fairly high quality," said the man. "I suppose I could give you seven hundred dollars for them."

Seven hundred. That wasn't enough. And Carter knew her father had paid closer to three thousand dollars for them.

She shook her head. "I know they're worth a lot more than that."

The old man sighed. "All right," he said. "Nine hundred."

"Fifteen hundred," said Carter.

The old man laughed quietly. "No, my dear. One thousand dollars. That is the most I will pay."

The man's expression was firm. Carter knew he wouldn't go any higher. She bit her lip.

"All right," she said. "One thousand dollars."

The old man took the earrings and slowly counted out ten hundred-dollar bills. She stuffed the money into the envelope that had once held her earrings. Carefully tucking it into her backpack, she went home.

She spent the rest of the afternoon in her room, trying to do her homework. But she couldn't concentrate.

She took the envelope full of money out of her backpack and opened it. She held the money in her hands, staring at it.

A thousand dollars. She was holding a thousand dollars in her hands. And she was about to hand it all over to Adam.

For what?

For a good score on her achievement test. For helping her get into Princeton—maybe. For making her father happy. For keeping it all a secret.

Was all that worth a thousand dollars to her?

It was. It was worth a thousand dollars, and a lot more.

* * *

Her father was late coming home from work. He was usually late these days. He couldn't leave the courthouse without being mobbed by reporters and photographers and curiosity seekers. The Henry Austin case was heating up.

So, the Phillips family ate dinner later than usual. The judge felt that it was important for the family to have that time together. He demanded that Carter and her mother wait to eat with him.

That night Mrs. Phillips didn't call Carter to dinner until after eight o'clock. Carter was starving by then. She hurried downstairs to the dining room.

Her father was already seated at the head of the table. Carter went over to him and kissed him hello. Then she took her place.

"How's the case going, Daddy?" she asked.

Her father frowned. Carter noticed how lined his face was.

"It's going well, I suppose," said the judge. "The prosecution's case is very strong."

"All the papers say they think he'll be convicted," said Mrs. Phillips. "He sounds like a terrible person. I think he actually *enjoys* hurting people."

"Yes," said the judge. "The facts that have come out of this trial are very troublesome."

He sighed. The stuffed fish was served, and Carter began to eat.

"Why don't we talk about something else," said

the judge. "How's the Spring Fling coming along?" He turned to his wife.

"I had a terrible time at my meeting today," Mrs. Phillips said. "Rita Weston may have a degree in design, but she has the *worst* taste when it comes to floral arrangements. . . ."

Carter tuned out. She hated to hear her mother drone on about her committee meetings.

She was lost in her own thoughts when she glanced up to reach for the butter and found both of her parents staring at her.

"Carter, didn't you hear your father?" said Mrs. Phillips. "He asked you a question."

"Oh. Sorry, Daddy. What is it?"

She turned to her father, so he could see that he now had her full attention. His face was red.

"Your earrings, Carter," he said. "Where are your earrings?"

chapter 11

Carter set down her butter knife. What was she going to tell him? Not the truth, that was sure. She had to put him off somehow.

"Oh, Daddy," she began, "I had such a scare today. I wore my earrings to school, like I always do. But after gym class, when I was changing in the locker room, I noticed that one of them was missing!"

Her father paled slightly and put down his fork. He lifted his napkin and wiped his lips. Mrs. Phillips didn't bat an eyelash.

"Did you find it?" asked the judge.

Carter could hardly bear the hurt on his face.

"Don't worry, Daddy," she reassured him. "I did find it. I spent ages looking for it, but it turned out to be stuck in the sleeve of my sweatshirt. It must have come off while I was changing."

Judge Phillips was obviously relieved and started eating again.

"But when I examined it, I saw that the back was loose. That's why it fell off so easily. So on my way home from school I took the earrings to a jeweler to get them fixed."

"You should have told me first, Carter. I would have taken them back to the place where I bought them. Which jeweler did you go to?"

Which jeweler? Carter racked her brain for the name of a jewelry store. She remembered the shop in the mall, the one with the necklaces she and Dan had checked out.

"I took them to that place in the mall—what's it called?—Sparkles, that's it."

Judge Phillips made a face. "I wish you hadn't done that, Carter. What kind of jeweler calls itself Sparkles? Will they do a good job there?"

"Oh, Daddy, I'm sure it will be fine. Stop worrying." Carter wished she felt as carefree about the whole thing as she sounded.

"When will they be ready?" asked the judge. "I'll pick them up for you. I don't want you to have to pay for this. After all, those earrings were a gift."

"No, you don't have to do that, Daddy. You and Mother are so busy these days. Besides, I'm at the mall all the time. I'll pick them up. I don't mind."

Nervously she watched her father, silently begging him to accept her excuses and lies.

The more he asked her, the more she had to lie. And with each lie she dug herself a deeper hole. She wanted him to believe what she said, but every time he fell for another lie she felt more and more guilty.

She could tell by the way he was eating, concentrating more on his food and less on her, that he was tired of talking about the earrings.

"All right, Carter," he said. He was focusing on his plate, picking out a fish bone. "I'll give you the money for the repair. Let me know what it comes to."

"Thanks, Daddy. I will."

She felt even more guilty now. He was going to give her more money. But she wouldn't turn it down. She knew she might need it—soon.

The next morning, on her way back from gym class, Carter passed a knot of kids in front of the cafeteria. Carter recognized most of them—they were in her grade—but she didn't know them well. They were the girls in secretarial programs, the guys in vocational, or kids who were just in the regular school track, not in honors classes like Carter.

All except for one. Adam was standing in the center of the group. He had his arm around a skinny, pale, freckled girl with light red hair. Sheila.

It was the first time Carter had seen them together since she'd gone out with Adam. The sight of them together was a bit of a shock. She wasn't sure why.

She'd always known that Sheila was Adam's girlfriend—Sheila wouldn't let her forget it. But somehow, she'd thought of the Adam she knew as a different person from Sheila's boyfriend. The Adam she knew wasn't going out with Sheila—he was going out with Carter.

He was a brilliant boy from the wrong side of the tracks, who wanted more out of life than his friends did. A boy who lived on the edge, who had a fierce sort of charm. Someone who could teach Carter things she had never learned in her plush, protected world.

Suddenly Carter saw that the Adam she thought she knew existed only in her mind. She'd made him up. He wasn't real.

This was the real Adam—the guy standing beside the cafeteria door with his shirt unbuttoned and his skinny girlfriend clinging to his chest. The guy surrounded by girls in tight jeans and purple nail polish and guys who cared more about what was under the hood of a car than what was in a girl's mind. The real Adam had tried to scare her with a bloody heart, to threaten her, and blackmail her, using her for everything he could get.

Now she hurried past this gang of kids, hoping Adam wouldn't notice her. She glanced back and saw him laughing and gazing in another direction, apparently unaware of her.

But then she noticed Sheila, standing cradled in the crook of his arm.

Sheila was staring at her with smug hatred, her small green cat's eyes gleaming.

"You lose, rich girl," her glare seemed to say.

Carter hurried down the hall.

After school that day Carter tucked the envelope full of hundred-dollar bills into her backpack and walked to The Corner. She knew that Adam was working that afternoon.

Carter took a seat at the counter, and Adam immediately came over to her. "I hope you've got something for me," he said.

She didn't answer him. She produced the envelope and slipped it over the counter to him.

He took it, but didn't open it.

"It's one thousand dollars, cash," Carter said. "Exactly what you asked for."

He put the envelope in his pocket. "I'll count it later," he said. "But it had better all be there."

"It is," Carter said firmly. "Now, I expect you to get out of my life, leave me alone, never speak to me again."

She stared at him, trying to intimidate him. He stared back, unwavering.

A man at the end of the counter shouted, "Hey! Can I get a menu, please?"

"Adam!" Carter said. "Did you hear what I said?"

"I've got a customer to take care of," Adam said. He walked away.

Carter grabbed her backpack and hurried out.

I've just given him a thousand dollars, she

thought. He's got to be satisfied with that. He's just *got* to be!

Carter didn't see Adam after she gave him the money, except during math class. And then he ignored her, pretended he didn't know her, just as before—before the test, the dates, before the terrible last couple of weeks.

At the end of school on Friday Carter breathed a sigh of relief.

It worked, she thought. Adam hasn't bothered me for three whole days. At last, he's out of my life. It took a thousand dollars, but I'm rid of him.

"Gary asked me what we did last Saturday night," Jill said. "I changed the subject, but what if he asks me again? Should I tell him the truth?"

Jill and Carter were standing outside the library, ready to go home for the weekend. Jill had a date with Gary that night.

"Don't tell him," Carter advised. "You don't know him well enough yet. You don't know how he'd react if you told him you went out with a guy like Ray."

"I hate to lie to him, though—" said Jill.

"You don't have to lie," Carter said. "Just be vague. Just say you and I went to some club in the Old Village to hear a band. He doesn't have to know more than that."

Dan came by. Carter flashed Jill a look that said,

THE CHEATER

"Shush—no more talk about this," and smiled at him.

"Hi, girls," Dan said.

Jill said, "I've got to go. I'll see you later, Carter."

"'Bye, Jill."

Carter and Dan started out of the school building toward the student parking lot.

"Doing anything tonight?" Dan asked her.

"Nothing," Carter said happily. "I'm free as a bird."

"Why don't you come over to my house? We can rent a movie."

"That sounds great." What a relief, she thought. No more lies. No more excuses.

She had her boyfriend back; she had her life back. She was so happy, she could hardly believe it.

After dinner she dressed to go to Dan's house. Nothing special. Still, Carter loved to put on a neat, clean, knee-length skirt and a yellow sweater. She topped it off with a blue ribbon in her hair.

I can wear anything I want! she thought happily. I don't have to try to look tough. I can be myself again!

She drove across North Hills to Dan's house, about a mile away. He opened the door for her and she kissed him hello. He looked beautiful to her in his chinos and blue polo shirt. She felt safe with him, she thought.

She walked into the living room to say hello to

89

Dan's parents. Mr. and Mrs. Mason had always liked Carter. Then she and Dan went downstairs to watch TV.

"I rented *Batman Returns* and *Wayne's World,*" Dan told her. "Which one do you want to watch?"

"*Batman,* definitely," said Carter. She'd already seen it, but didn't care. "I'm not in a comedy mood."

"Really?" said Dan. He had narrowed his eyes, studying her face. "Is there a reason?"

What was the matter with him? "What do you mean?" she asked. "A reason for what?"

"A reason you're not in a comedy mood."

"No," she said. "I just feel like watching *Batman.* Is there something weird about that?"

"No, no," Dan said hurriedly. He stooped to put the tape into the machine. "Of course not."

He sat beside her on the couch now, one arm around her, one hand holding the remote control. She snuggled against him and tried to relax.

What was *that* all about? flashed through her mind, but then the movie started and she forgot about it.

Still, every once in a while she thought she caught Dan glancing at her while they watched the movie, as if he were checking her reactions. The entire evening he seemed to be studying her closely.

Maybe he just feels insecure, she thought, when

the movie was over and they were sharing a dish of chocolate ice cream. After all, I turned him down for two dates in a row. He probably wants to be sure everything is okay between us.

She glanced up from the dish then, and smiled at him. As far as she was concerned, everything was great between them. After her experience with Adam, she never wanted to stray from Dan again.

To prove it to him, she put down the dish of ice cream and gave him a big, chocolatey kiss. Dan let his spoon fall to the floor.

They snuggled on the couch until midnight. Carter heard the Masons' grandfather clock strike the hour upstairs in the front hall.

"I'd better get going," she said, pulling her face just far enough away from his to speak. "You know Daddy."

Dan said, "I do." He gave her one last kiss, then stood and helped her off the couch. A short while later he walked her out to her car.

"Be careful driving home," he said.

They kissed once more. Then he closed the car door and stood in the driveway, watching her drive off.

Carter turned on the radio and hummed along to the soft music as she wound her way through the quiet streets of North Hills. She'd driven from her house to Dan's and back so many times she could practically do it in her sleep. Now, as she glided down the dark, curvy streets, she felt as if she were on automatic pilot.

Suddenly a harsh light was blinding her. She glanced into the rearview mirror and saw there was a car close behind her, its headlights on high.

I hate that, she thought irritably. She slowed and waited for the car to pass.

It didn't.

She sped up a little. The other car went faster too. It was tailing her.

She rolled down her window and gestured to the other car to pass her. The driver ignored her. The car stayed right on her tail.

She went faster; the other car sped up even more.

What's he doing? she thought. He's going to hit me!

The faster she drove, the faster the other car went. Her heart raced.

Who was it? What did they want?

She crossed a bridge and climbed a steep section of road that overlooked the river. Her speedometer read eighty. The other car was right behind her, pushing.

She couldn't go any faster. She was beginning to lose control of her car!

Cold with panic, her heart thudding in her chest, she heard the grinding sound of metal against metal. Her car was being nudged to the right.

"No!" Carter shrieked.

The other car was scraping her left rear fender—pushing her off the road!

"No!"

The car eased off, then hit her again. Her car lurched to the right.

Glancing down, she could see the river just beyond the low guard rail and over the edge of the steep slope.

She pressed the accelerator to the floor, desperate to outrun the other car. But it kept up with her, pushing and pushing. . . .

Who *is* it? Who is trying to kill me?

She raised her eyes to the mirror.

The white light nearly blinded her.

It's got to be Adam.

The steering wheel bounced under her hands. Her heart leaped to her throat.

The road curved to the left, the river out of view now. I'm safe, she thought. She jammed her foot on the accelerator and pulled ahead of the other car—just for a second.

It shifted to the right side of her car now. With a loud crash, it rammed into her.

"No!"

It was jolting her into the other lane. Into the oncoming traffic.

Carter gasped as she saw headlights ahead. Another car was roaring toward her.

The car behind her kept pushing, pushing, pushing her to the left, into the other lane.

"I-I'm losing control!"

The car began to slide.

Desperately she struggled to straighten the wheel.

Too late!

She screamed—closed her eyes—and waited for the crash.

chapter
12

With a heart-stopping jolt, her body slammed forward against the seat belt, then bounced back into the seat.

It took Carter a second to realize that she had stopped her car. She dropped her head on the steering wheel and shut her eyes, panting, waiting for her heart to stop racing.

When she opened her eyes, she saw out the side window that the oncoming car had swerved and come to a stop on the far side of the road. The other car—the one chasing her—must have sped away.

She heard a car door slam. Then she heard footsteps crossing the road toward her.

She lifted her head.

It was a man—a good-looking man in his thirties. He tapped on her window. She rolled it down.

"Are you all right?" he asked, squinting down at her.

Carter nodded. "I-I'm very sorry," she stammered. "The car behind me—it was driving too close."

The man frowned. "You'd better report that to the police."

"I will," she lied.

"What about your car? Is it okay?"

"I think so," Carter replied shakily. "Anyway, I think it will get me home. I live nearby." Then she asked, "What about you? Were *you* hurt?"

"No, I'm fine. Why don't you try to start the car, see how it works."

Carter nodded. She sat still for a minute, staring at the dashboard, still trying to catch her breath. Luckily for her, the car had ended up in a thick hedge beside the road and not wrapped around a tree or telephone pole.

She started up the car and slowly backed out of the bushes. "It seems fine," she told the man. "Thanks for your help."

He waved and went back to his car, shaking his head.

She drove home carefully, one eye on her rearview mirror, afraid that the other car would appear again. It didn't.

But when she pulled into her driveway, her headlights rolled over someone standing beside the garage, waiting for her.

Adam.

She parked the car and got out, slamming the door behind her.

"It *was* you!" she cried. She was furious. "I knew it! What were you trying to do, kill me?"

"Huh?" Adam acted confused. "I don't know what you're talking about. I don't want to kill you. No way."

"Then why were you chasing me?" Carter screamed. "Why were you—"

"I've been here, waiting for you," he interrupted. "I need more money."

She glared at him angrily, her chest heaving.

Was he telling the truth? Was it someone else chasing her?

"I don't have any more money," she said. "I just gave you a thousand dollars! That's all the money I had!"

"You can get more, Carter. Think about it. You've got lots of valuable things."

He gestured toward her luxurious house. "That place must be full of stuff you could sell. I bet there are plenty of things you could take that your parents wouldn't even miss."

"You're crazy!" Carter cried. "I can't steal from my parents."

"Why not?" Adam said coolly, grabbing her arm. "You've cheated on a test. You lied to your father and your boyfriend. I think you can handle stealing."

Her face burned. He let her arm drop.

"You've got until tomorrow night," he told her. "Bring another thousand to my house. If you don't, your father will hear from me on Sunday morning."

He walked down the dark driveway to his car, which was parked by the curb.

Carter stood on her front lawn, her head in her hands as he drove off.

It was hopeless. Adam just wouldn't go away. Her life was in his hands, and there was nothing she could do to stop him.

I could kill him. I could just kill him! she thought. She pictured herself grabbing Adam's pistol, shooting him. She saw him grabbing his chest. Then she pictured him falling in a puddle of blood.

"What am I *thinking* of?" she cried, horrified by her own fantasy.

But she knew there was no other way out.

chapter

13

The next morning Judge and Mrs. Phillips drove to a cousin's wedding in Waynesbridge.

"We won't be back until late," Mrs. Phillips told Carter. "I'm sure you can find something for supper in the freezer. If you need us, we'll be at the Chateau. I left the number by the phone."

"Okay, Mother."

Carter waved to her parents and was grateful she hadn't been invited to the wedding. She needed the day to figure out what she was going to do about Adam. It would be much easier without her parents around asking questions.

At eleven o'clock the doorbell rang. Carter went to answer it. She was surprised to find Dan standing on her doorstep. His expression was grave.

"Hi, Carter," he said. "Can I come in and talk to you for a minute?"

She stepped aside to let him in. "What is it?" she asked. "Is something wrong?"

"I'm not sure," he replied. "That's what I'm here to find out."

Carter gestured to her father's study and said, "Let's go in here to talk."

Carter stood leaning against her father's massive desk. Dan sat in one of the leather armchairs opposite her.

"I wanted to say something to you last night," he began. "But I didn't have the nerve."

"What is it?" Carter asked.

"Well," he said, "I've been talking to Jill." These words made Carter's stomach lurch. What had Jill told him?

"She's been worried about you, you know," Dan told Carter. "So have I. I could tell she knew something about what's been going on with you, about why you've been acting weird. So I decided to talk to her. I saw her at the club this morning."

Carter's face twitched nervously. "And—?"

"She told me some weird things. She told me how you said you cut your hand on a razor, but afterward, there was no cut. No bandage, no scar."

Carter glanced down at her hand. The bloody heart. She'd nearly forgotten about that.

"And she told me about your date with Adam and Ray—"

"Oh, my gosh!" Carter moaned. Dan's come to break up with me, she thought miserably. He's found out about Adam.

But Dan didn't look angry. He stood up now and put his hand on Carter's arm.

"Carter, I think I know what's going on. I didn't say anything to Jill about it, just in case I'm wrong—"

No, Carter thought. There's no way he could ever guess. How could he?

"You got Adam to take your math test for you, didn't you?" Dan said quietly. "And now he's blackmailing you."

He *had* guessed. Somehow, Dan had figured it all out. He knows me too well, Carter thought.

She had dreaded this moment. But now that it was here, Carter felt relieved.

At last! Someone she trusted knew the truth. She was so desperate to have her life return to normal.

Carter let her head fall on his chest. Then she broke down and told him the story.

Dan stroked her hair gently while she poured out the details. When she was finished, she looked up at him with tears in her eyes. "You must think I'm a terrible person," she said. "You must hate me."

But his eyes were tender.

"No, Carter," he said. "Of course I don't hate you. You made a mistake—that's all."

He stepped away from her now, and his expression hardened. He paced the room and said, "But I don't believe that creep Adam. Look what he's done to you. You're acting like you're about to have a nervous breakdown!"

All this time Carter had never thought about it

that way. Sure, Adam had done terrible things to her, but deep down she felt she deserved them.

"Listen, Carter," Dan said. "You've got to stop giving Adam money."

"I can't!" Carter heard her voice rising in panic. "I can't stop."

"You've got to do something, Carter. You can't let this go on."

"I won't let it go on," Carter said. "I'll find a way to stop him."

"How, Carter? What can you possibly do?"

"I don't know," she said. "But I can't stop giving him money. He's ruthless. If he doesn't get what he wants, who knows what he'll do!"

"Look, Carter," said Dan. "As long as you keep giving, he'll keep asking for more. It's got to end somewhere."

"I know, but what can I do? I can't stand it anymore, Dan. I can't stand him, and I can't stand what he's doing to me. He's taken over my life and he won't go away!"

She walked around her father's desk and pulled open a drawer. She slipped something out of the drawer. It was heavy and black. She hefted it in her hand.

A gun.

"If I had the guts," Carter said, "I'd kill him."

Dan raised his hands as if to shield himself.

"Carter, what are you doing? Put it down! Carter! Carter—"

chapter
14

Carter lowered the pistol, her angry fantasies lingering in her mind.

"Carter, what are you doing?" Dan's face became pale. "Where did you get that gun?"

"It's Daddy's," said Carter. "I found it here one day when he was out. He doesn't know I've seen it."

"Put it away," Dan snapped. He grabbed the gun from her and dropped it into the desk drawer. "That's not the way to handle a problem. It'll only make things worse."

Carter was shaking. "I just don't know what to do, Dan," she said. "I'm trapped. Totally trapped."

He held her, soothing her. "There's got to be a way out," he said. "Don't worry. Just stop giving him money. I'll try to think of something."

Carter leaned against Dan, glad he was there. She had never realized how strong he was, but even with his strength and calm, she couldn't imagine how he could help her out of this. She wished he could, but she knew it was impossible.

After Dan left, Carter hurried to her room. She took her jewelry box from the dresser and dumped the contents on her bed. Then she poked through it, picking out anything that could be of value.

She gathered together all the gold chains, necklaces, bracelets, and earrings, stuffed them in a brown paper bag, and drove to the Old Village.

Dan means well, she thought as she searched for a parking place. But he doesn't know Adam. If I can buy a little more time from Adam, maybe we can figure something out. But the important thing is to get Adam that money.

Adam could be really dangerous, after all. She remembered the terrifying car chase. Before that, the horrible double date. And before that, the cow's heart.

Adam's getting more dangerous all the time, she realized with a shiver. I hate to think what he'll do next.

She carried her brown paper bag full of jewelry into Corelli's Antiques.

Mr. Corelli remembered her. He smiled and nodded.

She dumped the jewelry on the counter, and the old man frowned.

"These items are not of the same quality as the earrings," he said with his accent. He sifted through it all carefully. Carter watched him impatiently.

Mr. Corelli picked out a few of the gold chains and bracelets. "I will give you two hundred dollars for these," he said, holding up the chains he had chosen.

Two hundred dollars! Carter needed a thousand. She tried to hide her desperation.

"Didn't you like these other things?" she asked. "I think you could sell them."

The old man shook his head. "No. Just these things. Two hundred dollars, miss."

Carter saw that he would not bargain this time. Maybe two hundred dollars would hold Adam for a few days, until she thought of some way to get more money. It would have to hold him.

"Okay," she said. "It's a deal."

Mr. Corelli gave her the money. She stuffed it into the paper bag and left.

She took the rest of the jewelry to the other antique shops on the block, but nobody wanted to buy the things Corelli had rejected.

Carter was near tears. What could she do? It was already five o'clock. She had no idea where she could scrape up eight hundred dollars on such short notice.

What would Adam do when she offered him only two hundred? Would he take it? Or would he be insulted, or angry that she couldn't give him all he'd asked for?

She didn't know how he'd react and was shaking with fear and fury as she made her way through the narrow streets of the Old Village to Adam's house.

Easing the car down Fear Street, she pulled up at the curb. Then she climbed out of the car, clutching her paper bag. She took a deep breath and walked up to Adam's front door.

It was dark by the time she turned onto her street. After leaving Adam's house, she had driven around in a daze, not seeing where she was going, and not caring.

One thought floated through her mind as she drove: Is the nightmare over now? Could it really be over?

Pulling into her drive, she saw that her parents were still out.

But someone was there, leaning against the front door.

Carter's heart pounded. She climbed out of the car and walked up to the front door. "Dan!" she cried.

"Where have you been?" he demanded.

She didn't answer him, avoided his eyes, and wondered why he'd come back. She opened the front door and went into the house. Dan followed her in.

"What's wrong?" he asked. "Did you see Adam?"

She didn't want to tell him. She tried to come up with another lie, something he'd believe.

She didn't get a chance. The doorbell rang.

With a cry of surprise, Carter went to answer it, Dan behind her.

She opened the door to two grim-faced police officers.

"Are you Carter Phillips?" asked one.

Carter stared at them, her mouth open. She nodded.

"We'd like to ask you a few questions."

"What about, Officer?" asked Dan.

The other police officer cleared his throat. "Someone shot Adam Messner," he said. "He's dead."

Carter froze. The police officers strode into the house, shutting the door behind them.

"Can we talk in there?" asked one, indicating the study. "We just have a few questions."

"Of course," said Dan. He led Carter into the room. The two officers followed. They all sat down.

Carter was glad Dan was there, handling this for her. He was so calm and collected. If only she could be that way. But she couldn't. She shook as she waited to hear what the officers had to say.

"Miss Phillips," said the first man, "this won't take long. Did you know Adam Messner?" He flipped open a notepad and sat with a pen poised above it, waiting for Carter's answer.

Carter nodded. "He went to Shadyside High. He was in my math class."

The other officer said, "Did you see Adam today, Miss Phillips?"

"No," Carter lied. Her mind was racing from thought to thought. "I know Adam, but we're not friends. I don't see him outside of school."

"One of his neighbors said she saw your car parked outside his house this afternoon," said the officer.

"No, she must have been mistaken," said Carter, shaking her head. "I haven't seen Adam today. In fact, Dan and I have been here all day, studying. Right, Dan?"

Dan looked at her, startled at first, and then suspicious. Then he backed up her story.

"That's right," he told the man. "We've been here all day."

"And where are your parents, Miss Phillips?"

"They're out of town at a wedding. They won't be back until late."

The officers glanced at each other, then stood up. The first one snapped his notepad shut.

"All right," he said. "Thank you, Miss Phillips. I hope we haven't upset you. We may have to come back later to ask more questions. But that'll do for now."

Carter showed them out. She shut the door after them, leaning against it with a sigh.

"You *did* go to Adam's house today, didn't you," said Dan, following her into the hall. "Why did you lie about it?"

Carter hesitated.

"I didn't want the police to get involved with my

troubles with Adam," she replied finally. "They might have found out why he was blackmailing me! But I didn't kill him, Dan, I swear it!"

Dan just stared at her.

Carter thought, I've never seen Dan like this before. So cold. What does it mean?

She strode up to him and grabbed his shoulders, pleading with him. "I didn't do it, Dan! You've got to believe me!"

But she could see that he didn't believe her. And Carter couldn't blame him.

After all, why should he believe anything she said? Lately, she'd done nothing but cheat and tell lies.

"I'm going home, Carter," Dan said, his voice strangely distant.

"Dan," she said, "will you call me later? I'll be here all alone for a couple more hours. I-I'm kind of scared."

He stared at her without smiling. "Sure, Carter. I'll call you later. Don't be frightened." But his words lacked any warmth.

He walked out without kissing her goodbye.

Alone in the house, there was nothing for her to do but pace from room to room. She walked upstairs, downstairs, upstairs, downstairs, thinking wild, frantic thoughts, her mind racing through the events of the past couple weeks.

As she paced, squeezing her hands into tight fists at her sides, one thought kept popping into her mind. She tried to push it out, but it wouldn't go away.

Adam is gone, she thought.

He's finally out of my life—forever.

My problems are solved.

Carter felt a brief moment of relief. But she couldn't enjoy it for long.

Because another thought intruded. Adam was dead, and the police knew there was a connection between them.

"What's happened to me?" she wailed out loud to the empty rooms. "I used to have a perfect life. How did it get so messed up?"

For an hour she paced the house this way. Finally the ringing of the telephone broke through her tortured thoughts.

It's Dan, she thought happily. It's Dan, calling to tell me he's sorry he doubted me, to make sure I'm all right. . . .

She answered the phone. "Dan?"

Another voice whispered, "Carter. I know what you did."

chapter

16

"**W**ho *is* this?"

Carter gripped the receiver with both hands. "Who *is* this?"

She heard a click, then dead air and a series of clicks. Finally a dial tone buzzed in her ear.

Carter dropped the phone with shaking hands. She was terrified.

Who could that have been? There was only one person she could think of—Sheila.

Carter started to pace again. What does Sheila know? she wondered, shuddering. Did Adam tell her anything—or everything?

Carter felt the panic rise within her. Sheila had been watching her, snooping around, hassling her since the day of the test. Was there something Sheila found out on her own?

Just then her parents' Mercedes pulled into the driveway. She ran upstairs and climbed quickly into bed. She couldn't face them now. Her father would be sure to see the guilt. . . .

A few minutes later Judge Phillips came into her room to check on her. Carter pretended to be asleep.

She spent Sunday in her room, telling her parents she wasn't feeling well. She had hardly slept the night before and couldn't sleep that day. She spent the day walking, pacing back and forth in her room, as if it were a prison cell.

She was exhausted when she got up for school on Monday morning. But she dragged herself out of bed and made herself go.

The best thing to do, she had decided, was to go on with her life as usual. Pretend there was nothing bothering her. Pretend everything was normal.

As soon as she got to school she realized how futile that was.

It was obvious that everyone in Shadyside had heard about Adam's murder. Carter stepped into the school building, smiling at her friends and saying hello to people, but that didn't last long.

No one smiled back at her. Her friends turned away—and the others just stared.

People stopped talking as she neared them. After she passed them, she heard whispering. She caught only a few of their words, but those few were enough:

"Police."

"Adam."

"Murdered."

Carter started walking faster down the hall, trying not to look into anyone's face.

Then she saw Jill. Her best friend. Carter ran up to her. But when Jill saw her coming, she became frightened and backed up a few steps. Then she turned and started to run.

Carter called after her. "Jill! Wait!"

Jill kept running. Carter started to chase her, then stopped.

She couldn't blame Jill for being scared of her, after all Carter had put her through. But they were best friends. . . .

She seemed to have become a freak, overnight. No one was on her side, not even Jill. She had no one—no one but Dan.

She had to find Dan. She had to find someone who believed in her. Someone who would help her.

He'd be upstairs, hanging out by his locker. She ran up the steps and down the hall. She saw him. He was alone.

She ran to him. "Dan!" she called.

He turned to her. One glance at his face stopped her cold.

He didn't smile. His eyes were ringed with dark circles. "Hi, Carter," he murmured softly.

He shifted his weight. He seemed uncomfortable with her.

Carter tried to ignore his coolness. She was

desperate for someone to talk to. "Dan," she said. "Why didn't you call me yesterday?"

He avoided her eyes. "I couldn't, Carter. I'm sorry."

Carter couldn't believe it. He's suspicious of me too, she thought. He's nervous around me, just like everybody else!

Dan was her last hope, and she grabbed him by the arm. "Please," she uttered in an urgent whisper, "not you too!"

She tugged at his arm, trying to get him to look her in the eye.

But he lowered his gaze to the floor. "I don't know what to say, Carter."

How can this be happening? Carter thought.

Dan is against me too.

chapter
——————
17

Carter made it through the rest of the day. She had no idea how. When she walked away from Dan, she just shut herself off. Turned her thoughts inward, away from everyone else. She avoided their eyes, didn't listen to their gossip.

She moved through the day like a zombie.

After a couple of days the kids at school stopped staring at her so much. No one talked to her, but at least they sat next to her in class now.

At home she jumped every time the phone rang, thinking it would be another threat. But the calls were never for her. Jill didn't call, and Dan didn't call. Sheila didn't call, either.

Maybe everything will be okay now, Carter thought. Slowly, my life will get back to normal. The kids will forget about Adam. Dan will relax and come back to me.

Maybe, Carter thought, the worst is over.

* * *

Then one evening Mrs. Phillips dragged the judge out to a charity benefit. Dressed in a sequined, silver evening gown, she came downstairs to the living room, where Carter was watching TV. Diamond earrings dangled almost onto her shoulders.

"Will you be all right tonight, Carter?" Mrs. Phillips asked her daughter.

Carter didn't take her eyes from the television set. "I'll be fine."

Mrs. Phillips sighed and cast a glance up the staircase. "What is taking your father so long?" she murmured. Then she shouted up the stairs. "John! We're going to be late!"

A few minutes later Judge Phillips appeared, adjusting the bow tie to his tuxedo.

"Why do we always have to be the first to arrive at these functions?" he grumbled.

"We have no choice, dear," his wife replied. "I'm the chairperson. I've got to be there first to greet all the guests."

"Next time you can go without me," said the judge.

"Oh, John . . ."

The judge paused in the doorway of the living room to say goodbye to Carter.

"We won't be late," he told her. "No matter what your mother says, I'll make sure we're back at a decent hour. I've got a lot of work to do tomorrow."

"Okay, Daddy," said Carter.

"Are you going to be all right here, all alone?" he asked.

"I already asked her that, dear," said Mrs. Phillips. "She says she'll be fine. Now let's go."

"Maybe you could ask Jill to come over and keep you company for a while," the judge suggested. "And remember, don't open the door to anyone."

Carter said nothing. She couldn't ask Jill, or Dan, or anyone else to come over and keep her company. They wouldn't do it.

"She can take care of herself, John," said Carter's mother. "Good night, dear. Don't stay up too late."

" 'Bye," said Carter.

She breathed a sigh of relief when the door finally closed behind them. Lately, she felt completely comfortable only when she was alone.

She microwaved a frozen pizza and sat in front of the TV to eat it. She had never watched as much TV as she had the last few days. There was nothing else to do.

After a couple hours Carter started to feel bored and sleepy. But it was only a little after nine. Too early to go to bed. She settled into the couch and clicked the remote control to see if she could find something better to watch.

Suddenly the television went off, and the lights flickered out.

"Hey—what's going on?" Carter wondered out loud.

She was sitting in complete darkness.

Carter sat up, alert. She thought she heard a noise.

Bump.

What was that?

Her heart jumped.

She listened again.

Another *bump*, followed by a scraping sound.

Someone was walking around in the house!

In the basement.

Call for help, she thought, panic rising in her throat.

She got off the couch and made her way into the kitchen.

Her hand hit the phone and knocked it off the hook.

She grabbed the wire and pulled the receiver up from the floor. Then she raised it to her ear.

The line was dead.

Frantically, she pushed the buttons.

Silence.

Dead.

She dropped the receiver when she heard a creak on the basement stairs. A footstep. Another. Coming up the stairs.

Terrified, Carter backed into the hall leading back to the living room. The footsteps slowly continued up the stairs.

Carter bumped into a small table. It fell over with a clatter. With a cry of panic, she kicked it aside and kept backing up.

The basement door opened.

"Who's there?" Carter whispered.

Now she heard someone walking toward her. Down the hall. Closer. Closer.

"Who's there?" she called out in a trembly voice she didn't recognize.

No answer. Just footsteps moving in on her, closer, closer.

Carter's back hit a wall. She stopped, pressing against the wall as if she could break through it.

The footsteps moved closer.

Now someone spoke.

"Careful—or you'll break Daddy's heart."

chapter
18

Adam?

No! No way. Adam was dead. But who else could it be?

"Adam?" she called.

No response. Another footstep. Another.

She struggled to see through the darkness of the windowless hall.

Adam? No. No. It couldn't be. Was it Sheila? Carter slid along the wall until she came to the door to the study. She backed inside.

The footsteps moved closer. The intruder was at the study door. She could make out a ski mask.

I'm trapped, Carter thought, trembling. I'm trapped. I'm—dead!

Her knees started to buckle as she backed up against her father's desk.

Then she remembered. The gun.

She stumbled around the desk as the footsteps moved into the room.

The intruder was almost upon her.

She felt for the top drawer and yanked it open.

With trembling hands she felt around for the gun. Where was it?

It was gone.

chapter
19

The intruder leaped at her.

Carter fell back, and the stalker lurched forward with a low grunt and pinned her against the wall.

She tried to scream, but he grabbed her by the throat, clamping his other hand over her mouth.

Carter knew this wasn't Sheila. He was too big, too strong.

It was a man.

A man with huge hands.

As she frantically struggled to free herself, he gripped her neck with both hands and squeezed her throat.

Carter gasped. All that came out was a squeak. I—I can't breathe, she realized.

She choked.

"You were a lucky girl," the man said in a low voice. "I tried to run you off the road, but you slipped away. Not this time. This time the message will get through. . . ."

He gripped her throat even harder.

Her lungs ached for air.

Stars began to dance before her eyes. He was choking her to death.

The stars grew brighter, brighter, until she couldn't see.

Then Carter was swallowed up by a blinding white light.

A faint wailing sound cut through the silence.

The wailing became a scream. Louder, louder.

The white gave way to flashing red lights. Sirens. Sirens! The police!

All at once the man's grip loosened on her throat.

Wheezing loudly, Carter sucked in a breath. The blood pumped back to her brain. She screamed.

The sirens were deafening now. From right outside the house.

The man's hands slid off her throat.

She was so dizzy. So dizzy. She screamed crumpled to the floor.

She heard a loud crash. Heavy footsteps.

The intruder started to run. Carter heard someone shout, "Freeze!"

Another voice cried, "I've got him!"

Carter sat up. The dark room was spinning. A flashlight beam bounced off the wall. Then the light hit her in the face.

"Hey. Are you all right?"

Carter blinked. Someone was helping her up. She raised her eyes to a worried-looking police officer.

"Miss?" he said. "Can you hear me? Are you hurt?"

Carter shook her head uncertainly. She opened her mouth to speak. Her throat hurt.

"I'm okay," she choked out.

"Can you walk?"

She nodded. She stared blankly into his worried face.

The officer supported her. He walked her into the hallway.

She stood before a knot of police officers. They had surrounded the intruder. He stood with his hands cuffed behind his back. He still wore the ski mask over his head.

Carter watched as one officer pulled the mask off.

Hesitantly, Carter stepped forward. The officer trained his flashlight on the man's face.

Carter gaped in shock.

chapter
20

*T*he man was sandy haired, heavyset, about forty-five years old. He had a craggy, ruddy face and thick, dark eyebrows. He scowled at her bitterly.

"Do you know this man, Miss Phillips?" asked the police officer.

Carter shook her head. "I've never seen him before," she said. "Who is he? I—I don't understand."

He knew her. She remembered what he had said. "Careful—or you'll break Daddy's heart."

Why had he said that? Had *he* been the one who put the bloody heart in her tennis bag?

He had also said that he tried to run her off the road. Then it hadn't been Adam, after all. Or even Sheila.

No. It must have been this man. This . . . stranger.

But why had he done it? Who was he?

Then Carter heard a familiar voice. "What's going on here? Where's my daughter?"

It was her father. Her parents were home.

"Here I am, Daddy!" she called. She ran to him and hugged him. Her mother leaned over to embrace her.

"Carter, what's happened?" she asked.

One of the police officers approached them. "Judge Phillips?" he said. "We're responding to a burglary call. Someone tripped the alarm in your basement door. We came as fast as we could. We heard someone scream, forced our way in, and found this man." He pointed to the intruder. "He attacked your daughter."

Carter's father held her tight. "Are you all right?" he asked her. "Did he hurt you?"

Carter shook her head.

Two officers began to lead the handcuffed intruder away. The judge stopped them.

"Wait a minute," he said. "I want to get a look at this man."

An officer beamed his flashlight on the intruder's face. The man glared angrily back at Judge Phillips, but didn't say a word.

"I recognize him," said the judge. "I've seen pictures of him. He works for Henry Austin."

Carter lifted her head. Henry Austin! What would he want with *me?*

"We're taking him in for questioning now,

Judge," said the police officer. "We'll call you if he tells us anything you should know."

Before all the officers left, one went downstairs to reconnect the electricity. The lights flickered on. The TV blared out. Carter switched it off.

She sat on the couch with her parents. Her father kept his arm around her, comforting her.

"Daddy," said Carter, "I don't understand. What was that guy doing here?"

"He's one of Henry Austin's thugs," said her father. "I think he was using you to try to send me a message. He wanted to scare me into letting Henry Austin go free."

Carter was confused. "What do you mean?"

"Austin's afraid the jury's going to convict him. He's trying to intimidate me—to get me to let him off. Honey, I'm truly sorry. I've often received threats. But it *never* occurred to me that anyone would ever come after you. You know I'd never intentionally put you in danger."

Carter nodded. She understood a few things now, things that hadn't made sense before.

Her father was studying her throat with concern. "Are you sure you're all right, Carter? Your neck is very red."

She raised her hand to her neck. It felt sore. But she didn't want to go to the hospital.

"It just hurts a little, Daddy," she said. "But I do feel a little weak. I think I'll go upstairs and lie down."

"All right, dear. I'll come up and check on you in a little while. I have to call the district attorney."

Carter slowly climbed upstairs to her room and shut the door. She lay on top of her bed covers to think.

All along, she had assumed that it was Adam who put the bloody heart in her tennis bag. Now she felt sure that it hadn't been him at all. It had been this thug who worked for Henry Austin. Why else would he have said "Careful, or you'll break Daddy's heart" when he attacked her? And he had confessed to being the one who tried to run her off the road as well.

Henry Austin was trying to intimidate Daddy by scaring *me,* Carter thought. He was sending Daddy a message: let Austin go or your daughter is dead.

Normally Carter would have told her father about the terrible things happening to her, but since she thought Adam was doing everything she couldn't.

I even thought it was Adam attacking me tonight, Carter thought, shaking her head. How dense can you get!

A detective came to the Phillipses' house the next morning. Judge Phillips greeted him and took him into his study to talk.

An hour later the door to the study opened. The detective shook the judge's hand and left. Then the judge called his wife and daughter into the study to tell them what the police had said.

Mrs. Phillips was very upset. The judge tried to calm her.

"The police questioned the intruder very closely last night," Judge Phillips said. "They got a lot of information from him, and they're holding him without bail. They assured me that we will all be perfectly safe now, and I believe them."

He looked at his wife who sat sniffling in her chair. She didn't say a word. She just shook her head nervously.

The judge sighed.

"Did he admit that he was working for Henry Austin?" Carter asked.

Her father nodded. "And Austin knows he was caught. Now that the police are onto him, I don't think Austin will try any more intimidation. At this point, it would hurt his case, not help it."

Carter's mother was still crying. She couldn't seem to calm down.

Carter watched her father as he took her mother's hand and held it warmly.

"Dear," he said, "the trial is almost over. When it's over, all this craziness will stop. Please stop worrying. Everything will be all right. I promise."

Mrs. Phillips stopped sniffling. She wiped her eyes and nodded.

"I trust you, dear," she said. "I trust you."

She climbed to her feet and made her way from the room. Carter watched her go. Then she stood up herself.

"Carter," said her father, "if you need anything, I want you to know I'm here for you."

"Thanks, Daddy."

She started out of the room, turning back toward her father as she shut the door. He took the gun out of his briefcase and put it back in the drawer.

That's why the gun wasn't there when I needed it, she thought. Daddy had it with him.

Slowly she began to feel safe. The thug was in jail. Adam was dead. The police hadn't questioned her about Adam's murder again. Things at school had calmed down. And she'd had no more mysterious telephone calls.

There was something else that made Carter feel better. Her father was making an obvious effort to reassure her that she was safe now. Although he was still very busy, he paid more attention to her. He made sure to ask her how she was feeling several times a day.

He feels guilty, Carter figured. After all, she'd been attacked because of his case. But Carter didn't care about her father's motives. She basked in his attention, and it did make her feel better.

It's really true, she thought happily. My life is going back to normal.

Three nights later Carter was studying in her room when the telephone rang. She answered it. "Hello?"

"Guess who, Carter? It's me. Sheila."

"Sheila—" Carter was too stunned to say anything else. Her sense of security melted away like ice in a fire.

"I need some money, Carter," Sheila said. "Five hundred dollars ought to do it."

"Huh? What are you talking about?" Carter asked. "Why would I give you money?"

"Don't play innocent. You know exactly what I'm talking about. You paid Adam to keep quiet, and now you're going to pay me."

"What? Why should I?"

"I'll tell you why. Because I know everything—I know all about you and Adam. Adam told me everything. Most of all, I know *you* killed him."

Carter's heart stopped. "I—I—"

"That's all right, Carter. Don't bother trying to deny it. I was the one who found Adam's body. I was the one who called the police. I know you killed him. And I've got proof."

chapter 21

Proof that Carter killed Adam? What proof could Sheila have?

Carter had to know.

"What are you talking about?" she asked Sheila in a trembling voice.

Sheila laughed. "No, Carter. It's not that easy. I don't give anything away for free. But don't worry—I won't hurt you as long as you meet me tomorrow night. Right behind Adam's house. At the edge of the Fear Street woods. And bring the money."

"Where am I going to get five hundred dollars?"

"You'll find a way. You always did before."

Carter swallowed hard. Sheila really did know everything.

"You give me the money," Sheila said, "and I'll give you the proof."

She hung up. Carter was left holding the receiver in a daze.

So much for things going back to normal. Her life was about to be smashed to bits again.

She hated the thought of seeing Sheila alone. She dreaded going back to Adam's house and dredging up all those awful memories.

But she had no choice. She had to find out what proof Sheila had—and she *had* to get it back.

Carter looked around her room, wondering where she was going to get the money. She had already sold all her valuable jewelry—and that had only brought half the amount Sheila wanted. What could she do?

Frantically, she dug through her closet. Clothes, shoes—nice things, but nothing that could command five hundred dollars on short notice. Her mother had a fur coat. . . . No, she told herself firmly. No. I can't take Mother's things, or Daddy's. They would never forgive me. This is my own problem and I've got to solve it myself.

She tried to concentrate, to see her room with fresh eyes, not to miss a single valuable possibility.

Suppose a thief broke in here, she thought. What would he steal?

Her eyes fell on her sound system—the CD player, amplifier, record turntable, and tape player. Of course.

It was a very expensive system, given to her by her parents for her sixteenth birthday. Even used, it might be worth a lot.

But her father would definitely notice its disappearance. How could she explain it?

I'll tell them it was distracting me from studying, she thought. I'll say I was spending too much time listening to music.

She imagined her father's grave face nodding in approval as she told him this.

Yes, she thought. That might work.

The next day she packed the whole system in a box and hoisted it into the trunk of her car. She drove to Marvin's Bargains, a store that bought and sold used electronic gear.

She lugged the box inside. The store was nothing more than a big warehouse, filled with used stereos, computers, appliances, even old records and tapes.

A middle-aged man in jeans and a vest looked the system over.

"How long have you had this?" he asked her.

"Just a year," she answered. She pulled a slip of paper from her pocket. "See, here's the receipt. My parents bought it a year ago." She was glad she'd remembered to dig out the receipt from her parents' files.

Please like it, she begged him silently. Please like it *a lot*.

"Everything working okay?"

She nodded vigorously. "Like a dream. It's the greatest, really."

"So why are you selling it?"

She hesitated. "Um, family emergency," she said. "I need the money."

He accepted this, and offered her three hundred dollars for it.

"Please," she pleaded. "I've got to have five hundred. I won't leave here unless you give me five hundred dollars."

The man looked at her in surprise.

"Look," Carter went on, holding the bill of sale under his nose. "Look how much my father paid for it. Only a year ago! You're getting a bargain."

He looked at the receipt again, and frowned. "Well, all right. I'll give you five hundred for it."

"Thank you!" Carter wanted to hug him, but she flashed him a happy smile instead.

That night she drove slowly down Fear Street. It was a dark, moonless night of long, shifting shadows, and Fear Street was even creepier than usual. The old Simon Fear Mansion loomed before her like a burned-out hulk. In the misty air, steam rose up from the remains of the house, so that it seemed to have burned just that day. Carter knew the mansion had burned years ago, but she felt as if something were alive in the ruins, some ghastly spirit that affected the whole street.

After tonight, Carter vowed, I'm never setting foot on this street again.

She passed the ruined mansion and parked her car a few doors away from Adam's house. Then she walked quickly to the house, her sneakers thudding nearly as loudly as her heart.

The windows were dark. No car in the driveway. No one home.

Carter felt a twinge of guilt as she passed the front door. A black wreath hung on it.

She crept through the yard, around the weed-strewn side of the house, and into the woods behind it. The Fear Street cemetery, she knew, lay nearby. Carter wondered if Adam had been buried there. Shuddering, she pushed the thought from her mind.

The mist grew thicker in the woods. Carter could see only a few feet in front of her. The trees became hulking, dark shapes, oozing moisture.

There was no breeze, no movement, no sign of life anywhere. Just the drip, drip of dew falling from the trees onto the mossy ground.

"Sheila?" Carter called softly.

No answer.

Carter shivered inside her jacket and leaned against a tree. She had the money in her pocket. All she could do was wait.

An owl hooted nearby. Carter heard the flutter of wings. Then she heard a *crack,* like the sound of a twig breaking. Dead leaves shuffling.

Footsteps.

The footsteps came from behind her. She spun toward the noise.

Squinting through the mist, she could hear some-one coming, but couldn't see anything.

Out of the shadows stepped Sheila.

She walked deliberately up to Carter, a smoking cigarette in one hand.

"The money," said Sheila, sticking out her free hand.

Carter began to reach into her pocket. Then she stopped.

"Where's the proof?" she demanded.

Sheila didn't flinch. "First, the money."

Carter pulled the wad of bills from her pocket and handed it over to Sheila.

Sheila smiled. She took two steps back from Carter and carefully counted the money.

"It's all there," Carter said impatiently.

"We'll see," said Sheila.

The money *was* all there, as Carter had said. Sheila smiled and stuffed it into her pocket.

"Now," said Carter. "What is this proof you have?"

Sheila pulled something out of her pocket and dangled it in front of Carter. It glimmered in the faint light.

"I found this on the floor of Adam's living room—right next to his body," she said. Her voice was hard and cruel and accusing. She said no more.

It was a gold locket. Carter took it from Sheila's hand. She examined it closely.

With growing horror, Carter recognized the necklace.

She opened it with trembling hands and gasped as she read the inscription.

"For Carter."

chapter

22

"*D*an. It's me, Carter."

"Carter—" She could hear the surprise in his voice.

It was Saturday, the day after she met Sheila in the Fear Street woods. Carter held the necklace between her fingers as she spoke to Dan on the phone. She watched it sparkle in the sunlight that poured through her bedroom window.

"My life is a mess, Dan," Carter said. "It can't get any worse, no matter what my father finds out about me. There's no point in keeping my secret any longer."

"Carter, what are you saying?" Dan sounded uncertain, as if he weren't quite sure what she was talking about.

"I'm going to talk to Daddy—today," Carter said. "I'm going to tell him everything."

"Are you sure about this, Carter?" said Dan.

Carter's voice was full of resolve. "I'm sure. Don't you think I should do it?"

"You should. Of course you should," Dan said quickly. "It's the right thing to do. I think you'll feel a lot better."

"I know I will," said Carter. "I just hope Daddy doesn't completely lose it. Dan, I need moral support. Somebody to help me get through this. Will you come over today? Daddy has always liked you, and you being here will give me the courage I need to actually go through with this."

Dan was silent.

"Please?"

"Of course, Carter," he replied. "I'd be glad to help you. I'll come over whenever you want."

"Thanks, Dan. Come over after lunch, okay? Daddy's always in a better mood after he's eaten."

"Okay. See you around two."

"I'll be here. Dan, thanks for staying with me through all this. It's meant a lot to me—it really has."

"I'd do anything for you, Carter. You know that."

Carter was waiting for Dan when the doorbell rang two hours later. She opened the door, took his hand, and pulled him into the house.

"Thank you," she whispered, squeezing his hand. "Daddy is in the study now," she said nervously.

"Are you ready?" he asked her.

She nodded.

They walked to the study. The door was closed. Carter knocked gently.

They heard the judge call, "Come in."

Hesitantly, Carter opened the door. She didn't step into the room, just put her head inside. "Daddy, are you busy?"

"Not really, Carter," said Judge Phillips. "Come on in."

Carter nodded to Dan. They stepped into the study and closed the door.

"Hello, Judge Phillips," said Dan.

Carter cleared her throat. "Um, Daddy, I need to talk to you. I—I have something important to say." Her voice came out high and shrill.

She glanced up at Dan. Her chin was trembling. He gave her an encouraging smile.

"I've done a terrible thing, Daddy," Carter stammered. "Actually, I've done a *lot* of terrible things. First of all, about the math achievement test—"

Her voice broke. She swallowed hard. "I'm sorry, Daddy. This isn't easy."

The judge said nothing. He kept his eyes trained on her and listened.

"I cheated on the math test, Daddy. I mean, I didn't take it over the second time. Someone took it for me." She paused.

"Who took it for you?" asked the judge.

"Adam Messner. He went to Waynesbridge and pretended to be me. He took the test in my place."

141

Carter lowered her eyes to the floor. Her hands were shaking.

The judge frowned severely. His face was hard. "So it was Adam who scored seven hundred thirty on your test, not you?"

Carter nodded. She glanced at Dan. He avoided her eyes.

"That's not the worst of it," Carter went on. "I have something else to tell you, Daddy. Something much more important."

The judge sat silently, waiting.

Carter took a deep breath.

"I did it, Daddy. I had no choice. He was blackmailing me."

The judge stared hard into her eyes. "Carter, you did what?"

"I killed Adam Messner."

chapter

23

Carter raised her eyes to Dan. He was staring at her, his mouth open.

But after a long moment, Dan composed himself. He crossed the room and stood in front of the judge's desk.

"Judge Phillips," he said, "you can help Carter, right? I mean, she's your daughter. You can deal with it, right? She won't have to go to jail, will she?"

The judge's face went slack. He remained silent. All the light faded from his eyes.

"I'm sure Carter didn't mean to do it, sir," Dan said, panic in his voice. "It could have been self-defense, right? Maybe it's not really murder."

The judge shook his head. "The courts will decide that. At her trial."

"No!" cried Dan. "Judge Phillips, you have to help her. You're a judge. You can do something. You can get them to go easy on her!"

"She took a life," said the judge. "That is a

terrible crime. So Carter must pay. She's my daughter, and I love her, but I won't use my influence in any way."

He paused. Then he sighed heavily. Carter waited to see what would happen next.

"There's no point in putting it off," the judge went on. "I'm sorry, Carter. I have to do this. I have no choice."

He picked up the telephone and started to dial the police.

Dan pressed his hand on the phone, cutting off the call. "Wait," he said. "I can't let you do this."

The judge set down the receiver. He raised his eyes to Dan.

"Carter didn't kill Adam," Dan said heatedly.

"What do you mean?" said the judge. "She says she did it. She just admitted it."

"No," Dan said. "She didn't do it. I don't know why she says she did."

"Well?" Carter's father demanded. "Then who did it?"

Dan cleared his throat. "I did."

With a loud sob, Carter ran to Dan and flung her arms around him. Dan pulled away gently and sank into the leather armchair.

"What's all this about? Please explain, Dan," the judge asked softly.

"I—I killed him," Dan said.

"Start at the beginning. Please," Judge Phillips said, folding his hands on the desktop.

"Adam was driving Carter crazy," Dan began. "He was blackmailing her, taking terrible advantage of her. He was holding this cheating thing over her head, threatening her with it every day. He was ruining her life. I hated to see her so miserable."

Dan stared at the floor. "I was worried about her too. Worried about her and me. I was afraid that Adam would get so tangled up in Carter's life that eventually he'd take her away from me. I know that's what he wanted."

Carter felt her face grow hot. It had almost happened that way.

"I begged Carter not to give Adam any more money. I begged her to stay away from him. But she was afraid of him, with good reason. And money was the only thing that kept him quiet.

"I thought that if I talked to Adam, maybe I could get him to stop bothering her. I had to try, anyway. So I drove to Fear Street, to his house that Saturday to see him.

"When I got there, I saw Carter's car pulling away. She had just been there. I knew she must have given him more money. I was so upset.

"I parked around the corner, so Carter wouldn't see me. I waited until she was out of sight. Then I walked up to Adam's house and rang the bell.

"I had no idea what I was going to do or say. All I knew was I was furious with him. He was ruining Carter's future—and mine too. Because I always thought Carter and I would be together."

He swallowed hard and looked at Carter. She sat across from him now, listening. She gave him an encouraging nod.

"Anyway, I had a feeling Adam wouldn't be very happy to see me, and he wasn't. I pushed my way into the house. I told him to stop blackmailing Carter and leave her alone. I told him not to bother her again.

"He grinned at me. He acted calm, but I could tell there was rage bottled up inside him. It was slowly coming to the surface.

"He said, 'Don't tell me what to do. I've got a good thing going with Carter right now—if you know what I mean. And it isn't going to end until I'm ready to end it. So run on back to your country club, kid.'

"That's when I really started to lose it. I felt so terrible for you, Carter. I was so sorry that you'd gotten mixed up with this creep.

"Then things got crazy. Out of control. I said, 'Today is the last you'll ever see of her, do you understand me? From now on you'll leave her alone!'

"He pulled away from me and took a few steps backward. He opened a drawer and pulled out a gun. He pointed it at me. I couldn't believe it.

"I never expected him to have a gun. I—I didn't think. I jumped him and wrestled him for the gun.

"There was a loud pop, and suddenly Adam grabbed his stomach and doubled over. His body— it crumpled to the floor.

"I glanced down. I was holding the gun in my hand. Somehow, it had gone off.

"When I turned to Adam, he was lying in a pool of blood. There was a big hole in his chest, and the blood was spouting up from it. Blood was everywhere.

"I—I freaked out. I just dropped the gun and ran."

Dan put his head in his hands and held it for a moment. Neither Carter nor her father moved. The room was silent except for the flapping of the window curtains. Outside, Carter could hear the drone of a lawn mower.

Dan lifted his head. He took a deep breath and went on.

"I was so panicky, I wasn't thinking straight. I didn't know where to go, or what to do. Somehow I found myself here. Some instinct told me I had to see you, Carter.

"But no one was home. So I waited. You didn't come home until after dark. I was going to tell you what had happened, Carter. I really was.

"But then the police came. I thought they came for me, but instead they questioned you. I was sure my fingerprints were all over that gun. But I guess after that struggle, they were probably so smeared up the police couldn't identify them."

He paused. Swallowed.

"And then you handed me an alibi, Carter," he said. "You didn't want the police to know about you and Adam, so you said you were studying with

147

me all day. You had no idea that I'd been to see him too. You had no idea that you were protecting me.

"I knew that if I confessed to killing Adam, all of your secrets would come out. Everyone would find out about the cheating. And you were so desperate to hide it. I started to think that maybe I could get away with it. Maybe we both could."

Carter glanced at her father. He was watching Dan.

"But I'd never let you take the blame for me, Carter," said Dan. "When I saw how much trouble you were in today, I had to confess. I'd never do anything to hurt you."

The judge leaned back in his chair, his gaze on Carter. She stood up and put her arms around Dan.

"See, Daddy," Carter said. "I was right. I told you he would do the right thing. I knew Dan would confess."

chapter

24

Dan gaped at Carter, confused. "Huh? What are you talking about?"

Carter stood up and carefully pulled something from her jeans pocket. The locket.

"Hey," Dan said, taking it from her. "Where did you find that?"

"Sheila Coss gave it to me," said Carter. "She found it in Adam's house—next to his body."

Dan raised a hand to his forehead. "It must have fallen out of my pocket while Adam and I were fighting."

"I recognized it right away, as soon as Sheila showed it to me," said Carter. "From the window of the jewelry shop. Remember?"

Dan had asked her which necklace she would choose, if she could have any of them. Carter had chosen the locket.

She smiled at Dan. "You had it engraved and everything."

Dan's face fell.

"When I saw the locket, I knew you had been there, Dan," Carter told him. "And I knew I couldn't let this thing go on any longer. So late last night I told Daddy everything. I told him about the cheating, the blackmail, the lies—everything. And I told him that I knew you had something to do with Adam's death."

The judge nodded. "I was ready to call the police right then and there," he said. "But Carter insisted you would do the right thing when the time came. She and I cooked up this little confession drama to test you, to see how far you'd go to protect yourself."

He paused. "You passed the test, Dan. I believe what you told us about Adam's death, and that you didn't mean to kill him. But we will have to talk to the police about this."

Carter stared intently at Dan's troubled face. Poor Dan, she thought. He's in all this trouble, just because of me!

She leaned forward on the desktop and asked, "What's going to happen to him, Daddy?"

"I don't know. But I think we can make a pretty good case that Adam's death was accidental, or at least that Dan acted in self-defense. After all, Adam was the one who pulled a gun on Dan. I'll do whatever I can to help."

Carter stepped around the desk to kiss her father now. "Thanks, Daddy."

Dan stood up and shook the judge's hand. "Thank you, sir. Thank you very much."

The rest of the day was a blur of activity. Judge Phillips took Carter and Dan to the police station, where they each gave their statements and answered endless questions. The judge found Dan an excellent lawyer.

Mrs. Phillips was horrified, of course, at having her daughter mixed up in such a scandal.

"They'll be dragging our name through the mud in the papers!" she cried tearfully at the dinner table that night. "I just hope they don't kick us out of the club!"

Carter rolled her eyes. The judge tried to comfort his wife. "Don't worry, dear," he told her. "They wouldn't dare kick us out of the club. Who would organize all their events?"

After dinner Carter went up to her room to change. She planned to go to Dan's house to hang out, to keep him company, and to talk things over.

She was brushing her hair when she heard a soft knock at her bedroom door. "Come in," she said.

Her father opened the door and walked in. "Hello, dear," he said. "May I sit down for a minute?"

Carter nodded. Her father sat beside her on the bed. He cleared his throat and tugged at his collar, as if it were too tight. Carter realized she'd never seen him look so uncomfortable.

"I came to apologize to you, Carter," he began. "I had no idea that you felt so much pressure in school, and I think it's mostly my fault. All that talk about Princeton, and my demands about your test scores. What I really meant to do was show you how much confidence I had in you. I had no idea I was pushing you so hard. I'm very sorry."

Carter gave him a warm smile. Her father smiled back. He put his arm around her.

"The next time something is bothering you, or you have a problem, please come and tell me," he said.

"I will, Daddy," said Carter. "I promise."

Carter was sitting on the floor at Dan's house, a chess board spread out between them. Dan moved his queen.

"Check," he said.

Carter groaned. "I can't believe it. You're beating me at chess!"

"That's only because you didn't cheat this time," Dan said. "What's going on? You *always* cheat at chess."

Carter moved her pawn. "I think I've learned my lesson," she said.

Dan glanced at the board and smiled. Then he moved his queen again and said, "Checkmate!"

About the Author

"Where do you get your ideas?"

That's the question that R. L. Stine is asked most often. "I don't know where my ideas come from," he says. "But I do know that I have a lot more scary stories in my mind that I can't wait to write."

So far, R.L. has written nearly three dozen mysteries and thrillers for young people, all of them bestsellers.

R.L. grew up in Columbus, Ohio. Today he lives in an apartment near Central Park in New York City with his wife, Jane, and thirteen-year-old son, Matt.

THE NIGHTMARES NEVER END . . . WHEN YOU VISIT

Next . . . SUNBURN
(Coming June 1993)

Claudia Walker thought spending the week with her friends, getting the perfect tan at Marla Drexell's cliffside beach house, would be fun. And at first it is. The luxurious house is on a beautiful, deserted strip of land, and the girls are pretty much left to care for themselves.

Then strange things begin to happen. Mysterious shadows are seen in the guest house. Horrible accidents occur on the beach and in the house.

Claudia knows they're not "accidents." She's sure somebody is out to get them . . . out to kill them. Their week of "fun in the sun" has turned dark and deadly!